UP A TREE IN
WITH

This is P. Robert Smith's first novel.

P. ROBERT SMITH

Up a Tree in the Park at Night with a Hedgehog

VINTAGE BOOKS
London

Published by Vintage 2009

2 4 6 8 10 9 7 5 3 1

First published in Great Britain by Vintage
Vintage
Random House, 20 Vauxhall Bridge Road,
London SW1V 2SA

www.vintage-books.co.uk

Addresses for companies within The Random House Group Limited can be
found at:
www.randomhouse.co.uk/offices.htm

The Random House Group Limited Reg. No. 954009

A CIP catalogue record for this book
is available from the British Library

ISBN 9780099522997

Typeset by Palimpsest Book Production Ltd,
Grangemouth, Stirlingshire

Printed in the UK by CPI Bookmarque, Croydon CR0 4TD

For Fran
For Mum and Dad
For everything

1

'What's wrong?'

'Nothing,' I lied.

'Are you sure?' she asked.

'Well . . .' I said.

'What is it?'

'This is going to sound really weird.'

I was with Cherry. We were on my bed, naked. It was also the *first* time we'd been on my bed naked. In fact, it was the first time Cherry had been on *any* bed naked – at least with anyone else. She was, unbelievably, not only incredibly, incredibly beautiful, but also a virgin.

This took some getting used to.

'What is it?' she asked again. 'Am I doing something wrong?'

'No, of course not,' I told her. 'You're fantastic! You're wonderful! You're gorgeous! . . . It's just that . . .' – how could I put this exactly – 'do you think you could maybe stick your finger up my arse?'

She stared at me like only a naked Korean virgin just asked to stick her finger up her teacher's arse could.

'*Pardon?*'

'I know it's a bit of a strange request, but I wouldn't ask if it wasn't important.'

'Is it usual?' she asked innocently.

Bless her. 'Well, not exactly,' I said.

When I first saw her naked, about five minutes before I asked her if she could stick her finger up my arse, I literally went weak at the knees.

'Which finger?' she asked me.

'It doesn't matter,' I said. 'Well, maybe the middle one.'

I don't mind admitting that it was an embarrassing thing to have to ask, but it would have been worth it – the effect was instantaneous and dramatic – if only what happened next hadn't happened.

———

'See you tonight, baby.'

Cassie planted a soft kiss on my forehead, and I mumbled something unintelligible back. I had no idea what time it was, but if Cassie was leaving for work it had to be unspeakably early. Civilised people had no business being up (or waking others up) at such an hour, I thought grumpily, as the door closed behind her and I rolled back over into oblivion. But not for long. Seconds later (or so it seemed), a submarine, obviously in dire danger, incongruously decided to submerge in the general vicinity of my bedside table. 'Dive! Dive!' I could almost hear its skipper cry, as the ungodly klaxon of my alarm clock exploded in my ear. I hit the snooze button. I hit it again. And again. Finally I stopped hitting it and managed to focus my eyes on the actual time.

'Shit!'

I leapt out of bed and into the bathroom. I was halfway through shaving, one side at a time, so that I had a perfectly shaven half-face, and a perfectly unshaven half-face, when my electric razor stopped.

'Shit!'

I shook it; I switched it on and off. I jiggled the plug, clicked off the front and emptied a week's accumulated shavings into the sink. Then I tried all of the above again.

Nothing.

Dead.

I looked at my reflection in the mirror.

'Shit!'

I figured Cassie had to have some razors kicking about some place. I looked in the cupboard under the sink. Tampons. I pulled out drawers. More tampons. I looked in the shower – no tampons, but no razors either.

'I don't believe it.'

I looked at the time.

'*Shit*!'

———

The man behind the counter didn't say anything, but he didn't need to. His evil, ear-to-ear grin said it for him. And when he saw the packet of disposable razors lying on his counter, it was all he could do to half suppress the giggle of near manic delight which was bubbling dangerously away just below the surface of his respectable shopkeeper façade.

'Just these,' I told him.

'No shaving cream?' he asked, wrestling heroically with his straight face.

I knew he was trying to be funny, but he had a point. 'Oh, yeah. I'd better have some shaving cream as well,' I said, and scurried back to the shelf to get some.

'There's gel if you prefer,' he called out to me. 'Some people like it better than shaving cream. Less messy. I use an electric razor myself.'

'Really?' I said, plonking it down next to the razors. 'That's very interesting.'

'Oh, yes,' he continued leisurely, thoroughly enjoying himself. 'I'm a bleeder. Cut myself shaving and I pass out through loss of blood. It's horrible. You'd think you'd stumbled into a slaughterhouse or something.'

'Actually, I'm in a bit of a hurry,' I told him. 'I'm late for work.'

'Oh yes? What do you do?'

'Sorry?'

'What do you do? For a job, I mean.'

'I'm an astronaut.'

'Is that a fact?' he said, ringing up my purchases. 'So is it true that in space when you cut yourself shaving no one can hear you scream?'

I paid, picked up my razors and shaving cream and gave him my best 'I'm so glad you find it amusing' smile.

'I'll let you know,' I said.

———

I collapsed at my desk. I had exactly forty-seven seconds to prepare my lesson, and I hadn't even had a cup of tea yet.

'Cut yourself shaving?' Fiona asked.

'Only a couple of hundred times,' I told her. 'I think I was sold a packet of rusty razor blades.'

'You should try an electric razor. They're really good.'

2

My brother drives a black cab. The first time he picked Death up he didn't realise it was him until after he'd jumped in. It was raining heavily at the time, and Ray hadn't noticed the flapping black shroud and scythe. He probably wouldn't have picked him up if he had, but then again a fare's a fare. He's a regular customer now. In fact, my brother's become a sort of unofficial driver for him. Nothing's ever pre-arranged or anything, Death just seems to pop up a lot when Ray's passing.

'What do you talk about?' I asked him when he first told me.

'He's not particularly chatty,' he said. 'In fact he doesn't say diddly. He just slips me a piece of paper with an address on it and says, "Drive". I drive there and wait outside until he comes back. With the meter running of course.'

'Isn't it a bit creepy?' I asked him.

'Not really,' he said. 'Everybody's got a job to do, haven't they?'

———

My brother doesn't need to drive a cab. He's a writer – *was* a writer. He once wrote a book about a rubber duck called *The Adventures of a Rubber Duck*. It was, surprisingly, a bestseller. I say surprisingly because it wasn't, as you might expect from the title or the main character, who was indeed a rubber duck, actually a children's book, but was in fact a rather dense and allegorical novel that came in at just under five hundred pages. A hefty read. And not only did it come in at just under five hundred pages, but my brother left it open-ended, thinking he would finish it off in a sequel, or perhaps even expand it into a lucrative trilogy. On the subject of rubber ducks, he obviously had a lot to say.

The sequel, however, was destined to leave his recently acquired legions of fans disappointed. Actually, disappointed wasn't the word. Furious. That was the word. The sequel left his recently acquired legions of fans furious.

Personally, I rather liked it. It was called *The Further Adventures of a Rubber Duck*. The reason it made his fans so furious was simple: It wasn't quite what they were expecting.

It was a children's picture book. He even did the illustrations himself.

It too was left open-ended, but this time his erstwhile fans were not clamouring to know what happened next. As far as his ex-fans were concerned, my brother, and his rubber duck, could both go to hell.

And that, as far as his writing career was concerned, was that.

————

The strangest passenger Ray ever picked up (apart from Death) was a beautiful naked woman who, when she got out, handed him a fifty-pound note. The fare was under a tenner, but when he went to give her the change she wouldn't take it. Being independently wealthy as he was, however (and perhaps succumbing, understandably, to the natural desire to try to impress a beautiful naked woman), he insisted.

'But it was a fifty,' he said. 'I couldn't possibly keep it.'

'Look at me,' she said, needlessly. 'Where would I put it?'

———

Ray's girlfriend is a doctor. Her name's Zadie. She used to be a lawyer, but she had an experience – an epiphany, I guess you could call it – which caused her to reconsider her career choice, and subsequently take up medicine.

Like many epiphanies, it happened in a bar. A man was choking on a honey-roasted peanut and Zadie, without apparently ever having seen it done before, grabbed him from behind and performed a life-saving and text-book example of the Heimlich Manoeuvre on him.

The man choking on the honey-roasted peanut was my brother.

He was at my stag night.

3

My wife-to-be, Georgia, fell off a ladder while trying to climb through an unlocked upstairs window after losing her keys on her hen night. She broke her leg. She also broke her neck, which was more serious. Not that it was fatal. However, unable to move or even cry out for help, she subsequently froze to death during the night.

———

She was my childhood sweetheart. We grew up four and a half minutes away from each other in one of the less interesting parts of Stoke. She was also the first girl not related to me to see my penis. We were eight years old.

'It's tiny!' she squealed.

'Is it?' I said.

'I've seen much bigger.'

'You have?' I said. 'Whose?'

'My dad's,' she replied proudly.

I was impressed. 'You've seen your dad's wing-wang?'

'Yes,' she said. 'Mum was having a drink out of it.'

———

It was another four years before she reciprocated and showed me hers. I just looked at it. I didn't know what to say.

'It's nice,' I said at last.

'Thanks.'

'You're welcome.'

She seemed reluctant to put it away, so I tried to think of something else to say. 'Does it do anything?'

She looked at me funny. 'Wuddaya mean?'

'I don't know,' I said, and I didn't. 'Can you put stuff in it?'

'It's not a pocket,' she said. Then she told me to lick my finger.

'What?'

'Lick your finger,' she repeated.

I was instantly suspicious. 'Why?' I asked her.

'I wanna show you a trick.'

———

It was a good trick, but it turned out she had an even better one up her sleeve. She showed me this new trick in the park under the old steamroller whose still movable gear stick I had once, and not that long ago either, derived so much enjoyment from jiggling back and forth.

'You have to take out your sausage,' she told me.

'Why?'

'Because.'

I couldn't argue with her reasoning, so I took it out.

'Now rub it.'

'What for?'

'To make it go hard, stupid.'

While I dutifully did as I was told, she casually hoisted up her skirt, pulled down her panties, and lay back with her hands behind her head and knees apart.

'Now put it in,' she told me.

'In *there*?'

'It'll feel nice.'

'It won't fit.'

'Yes it will,' she said.

'No way!'

'Betchitwill.'

'How much?'

'50p.'

'OK,' I said. '50p.'

'Shake,' she said.

We shook.

I lost the bet, although I didn't really mind that much. And she was right about something else too. It did feel nice. Very nice. In fact it was just starting to feel so nice that I thought something unbelievably wonderful – although I had no idea what – was about to happen, when an old lady bending down to investigate her dog's doo spotted us and spoiled our fun.

'*Hey*!' she called out to us. 'Cut that out, you little perverts!' (Neither one of us knew what a 'pervert' was, but I later looked it up in a dictionary and heartily agreed.)

We both pulled up our clothes and ran for it. When we finally stopped, we burst out laughing.

'Do you think she saw what we were doing?' I asked, gasping for breath.

'Of course she did,' said Georgia. 'She's probably telling the police right now.'

'The police?' I said. 'What for?'

'It's against the law, silly.'

'Is it?'

'Of course. Otherwise everybody'd be doing it.'

'Can you go to jail?'

'If you get caught.'

This was a bit worrying. 'Do you think she'll be able to recognise us?'

'Well, maybe not your face,' said Georgia, and giggled.

I looked down. I hadn't noticed before, but my little prick was still rock hard, straining against my shorts.

'You've still got a stiffy,' she giggled.

'What'll I do?'

'You'll have to pull it.'

'What for?'

'To make it go down again.'

I didn't understand the logic of this at all.

'What if I just leave it? Will it go down then?'

'I guess.'

'How long will it take?'

She shrugged.

'You don't know?'

'Well, I haven't got one, have I?' she said.

'What if you pull it?' I suggested.

'Sorry,' she said, 'I'm already late. Mum's gonna kill me.' And she darted across the road in the direction of her house and was gone.

———

I walked the streets for another hour waiting for my erection to go down. When it finally did and I got home, my mother said, 'Look at the time, young man. Where have you been?'

'Nowhere,' I said, and went upstairs and lay down. My balls ached.

11

4

I'm not saying Georgia falling off a ladder and dying of exposure was necessarily a good thing, but then again, looked at a certain way, it did rather effectively prevent me from making what with hindsight I can only say would have been a hideous mistake.

My brother, Ray, broke the news to me the following morning. I was asleep on his couch when the phone rang. He stumbled out of his bedroom and answered it. I don't know whether the blood drained from his face when the voice at the other end told him the tragic news or not, as I was too busy suffering the first shock waves of my hangover, but it probably did.

'Ben,' he said. 'I've got some pretty bad news.'

'Don't tell me,' I said. 'She's called the whole thing off?'

'Well,' he replied, sitting on the edge of the coffee table in front of me, 'in a way, yes.'

I sat up despite the throbbing in my head.

'What do you mean?'

'There's no easy way to say this,' he continued, 'so I'll just come right out and say it.'

I waited.

'Well?' I said.

That's when he burst into tears.

'She's dead,' he sobbed.

'Who is?'

'Georgia.'

'Georgia?'

'I'm sorry.'

'Georgia's *dead*?'

'She fell off a ladder last night while trying to climb through an unlocked upstairs window.'

'What!'

'She broke her neck.'

'Oh my God!'

'But that's not what killed her.'

'It isn't?'

'She froze to death.'

'She broke her neck *and* froze to death? Jesus Christ!'

And that's when he said, and I do appreciate he was trying to be kind, perhaps the stupidest thing I have ever heard anyone say in my entire life.

'I'm sure she didn't suffer.'

I just stared at him.

'What?'

He repeated his kindly assurance.

'Have you ever broken your neck or frozen to death?' I asked him.

'No,' he admitted.

'Neither have I,' I said, 'although I'm pretty certain it can't be pleasant.'

'It's better not to think about that.'

'OK,' I agreed. 'What about watching some TV? There might be a good cooking programme on.'

'It's OK, Ben,' he said reassuringly. 'You're in shock.'

'No I'm not,' I told him.

'That's just what people in shock always say. It's a sure sign.'

'Of what?'

'Of being in shock.'

He was probably right, of course. I probably was in shock. At least, I would never ordinarily suggest watching a cooking programme. And after that, after recovering from the shock, or from suddenly acquiring a taste for cooking programmes, people naturally enough assumed I was heartbroken.

But I wasn't.

I was upset, but definitely not heartbroken. This took me somewhat by surprise.

———

'I think there's something wrong with me,' I said to Jamie one day on the bus. He looked up from doing his nails and said, 'Why?'

'I don't feel bad enough.'

'About Georgia?' he asked, blowing on them now.

'Yes.'

He admired his handiwork a moment, as well he might. He had very nice nails. He'd always had nice nails, even at school where they'd been the envy of all the girls (his range of day-glo polish was legendary) and one of many, many reasons for routinely having the crap beaten out of him by all the boys.

'How *do* you feel?'

'Upset,' I said.

'But not heartbroken, right?'

'Right.'

'I wouldn't sweat it,' he told me. 'You've got plenty of life left for heartbreak.'

The little girl sitting in the seat in front of us who'd

been sneaking peeks at Jamie for the last three stops suddenly swung right round in her seat to confront the object of her ardent fascination face to face.

'Can I help you, little lady?' Jamie asked her.

'Excuse me,' she said politely, 'but are you a lady or a man?'

'*Jennifer*!' snapped her until-now unheeding mother, her jaw having just hit the floor and bounced back again.

But Jamie just flicked his long blond wig and replied, with aplomb, 'Neither, honey. I mean, why be a noun when you can be an adjective?' leaving the little girl none the wiser, perhaps, but me in no doubt whatsoever what that adjective might be.

Fabulous.

———

Jamie, when he spoke of there being plenty of life left for heartbreak, knew what he was talking about. He'd always felt guilty about his mother's death, which, considering she died of a heart attack brought on by unluckily selecting one of her as-far-as-she-was-concerned straight son's gay orgy photo albums for a casual perusal while he busied himself in the kitchen making them a cup of tea, was understandable.

'Hob-Nob, Mum?' he'd called out. 'They're double choc.'

He found her sitting where he'd left her, the smoking gun, or in this case cardiovascular-popping photo album, still on her lap. It was opened at a particularly imaginative and eye-watering tableau.

He knew she was dead instantly, and has never understood how or why he didn't drop the tea-and-Hob-Nobladen tray he was carrying. 'People do, don't they – in movies?' he asked me shortly after it happened, and has continued to ask at regular intervals ever since. As it was, he put the tray down on the coffee table in front of his now wide-eyed dead mother, collapsed into the chair opposite, and slowly but devastatingly fell apart.

5

I don't know why exactly I say getting married would have been a hideous mistake. Perhaps because neither one of us really had any life experience other than what we'd experienced together. After all, we'd effectively been a couple since the age of eight, which hadn't really left too many windows of opportunity. We hadn't even slept with anyone else – or rather, I hadn't slept with anyone else, and Georgia only had the one time, and then by accident.

We were at a party.

We were seventeen and, like most seventeen-year-olds at a party, we were extremely drunk. And like most seventeen-year-olds at a party who are extremely drunk, our thoughts – never far away anyway – turned to sex.

We made our way upstairs to an unoccupied bedroom, where Georgia, writhing and twisting free of her clothes, toppled in a drunken and extremely inviting heap on the bed. Unfortunately the room chose that precise moment to begin rotating at speed, and I staggered off somewhere to be violently sick all over myself and my surroundings.

Now, due to a series of hazy and barely creditable coincidences, Georgia's younger brother, Roger, who also happened to be at the party, found his way, independently and unintentionally, to the same bed, in the same darkened room, in the same advanced stages of

17

drunken stupefaction and, as it turned out, sexual receptiveness. I have no doubt he was merely looking for a place to lay his spinning head, but it didn't take long for the first dazed and drunken sounds to turn to moans of mounting drunken pleasure as the two of them proceeded to get a little more intimately acquainted than is generally deemed acceptable between siblings.

They were still there in the morning when I at last found my way back to the room after spending the night with a mouthful of carpet.

As I stood at the foot of the shambolic bed, mouth agape, looking down at the naked figures sprawled amongst its wreckage, Georgia opened her eyes.

'Hey,' she said.

'Hey,' I said back.

Then she looked down at the hand cupping one of her breasts. Her brow furrowed, and she turned around to see her brother lying beside her. A little pool of drool had gathered on the pillow by the corner of his mouth. He was sleeping like a baby.

'What the – ?' she said.

And then, in answer to her own half-asked question, she screamed.

———

I had sex for the first time with someone other than Georgia exactly two days after her funeral. I was feeling bad about not feeling worse so I went to a bar and got drunk and met a not very attractive and particularly undiscerning woman who, to illustrate just how undiscerning she was, was actually willing to sleep with someone like me.

We went back to her place and did it.

When we were finished I lay on my back and stared at the ceiling. It was so totally unremarkable that I could have stared at it all night, except that Linda – that was her name – appeared intent on furthering our relationship through post-coital conversation. Personally I had very little to say, and would have been more than happy to continue to lie there on my back staring at that hypnotically unremarkable ceiling. I think, perhaps, I'd been hoping for an all-consuming and soul-crushing guilt, but by the time I rolled off I would have been happy with even the mildest twinge.

'So, am I going to see you again?' Linda asked, nibbling my earlobe.

'To be honest,' I told her, 'I don't think so.'

The nibbling stopped. Instantly.

'You could at least lie, you arsehole,' she said, and rolled away from me.

I hadn't exactly meant to say what I said, which of course didn't make it any less cruel or hurtful, and I instantly felt that sharp twinge that had earlier eluded me.

'I didn't mean it that way,' I said.

'Whatever,' she replied, snuffling softly.

'No, I mean it,' I said. 'It just didn't come out right. I think you're a very nice person. You're friendly, outgoing –'

'Yeah, thanks.'

'It was my fiancée's funeral two days ago and I guess I'm still a little messed up,' I said.

She sat up and looked at me, all wet and smudged. 'What?'

'We were supposed to get married on Saturday.'

'You're kidding?'

'It's true. We were childhood sweethearts. You're only the second girl I've ever had sex with.'

She was looking at me a little too intently now. 'How did she die?' she asked.

'She fell off a ladder while trying to climb through an unlocked upstairs window after losing her keys on her hen night,' I told her. 'She broke her neck and froze to death.'

'Jesus,' she said.

'That's what most people say.'

'No, I mean I knew her.'

'You knew her?'

'Georgia, right?'

'Right.'

'Jesus,' she said again. 'I was going to your wedding.'

———

About a week later there was a knock on my door and I opened it to find Roger, Georgia's brother, standing there. I hadn't heard from him since the funeral and I was pleased to see him. I'd known him as long as I'd known Georgia, and although I was now the only other living person who knew he'd slept with his own sister, we were friends, and I knew he had taken Georgia's death very hard. At the funeral itself, and leading up to it, as bad as he was obviously feeling, he'd done every-thing possible to try to comfort me, which of course had the completely opposite effect, making me feel like a worthless, stony-hearted, unfeeling dog. He also said the equally most stupid thing I've ever heard in my entire life, which was this:

'I know she'd want you to be happy for her.'

This made so little sense on so many levels it was simply beyond reply, so I didn't. I just watched the coffin being lowered into the ground and tried not to hum the song that had been going round my head all morning since I'd heard it on the radio while taking a bath. It was Katrina and the Waves' 'Walking on Sunshine' which, incidentally, has one of my all-time favourite guitar bits, but which was still, in spite of this, spectacularly inappropriate humming material for a dead fiancée's funeral.

'Rog–' I said, before being interrupted by his fist connecting with the middle of my face. When I looked up at him from my new position on the floor, a hand cupping the stream of blood flowing from my broken nose, I could hardly reconcile the angry and contorted features I saw in front of me with those of the gently supportive and bravely bereaved Roger of a mere week ago.

'You piece of shit,' he said.

'I think you've broken my nose,' I said.

'I should break your fucking neck, you bastard!'

'I don't know what it is you think I've done, Roger,' I told him, 'but whatever it is I promise you I didn't do it.'

'Are you telling me you *didn't* sleep with a girl called Linda Paxton two days – *two fucking days* – after we buried *my* sister and *your* fiancée? A week before you

21

were supposed to *marry* her? Is *that* what you're telling me, Ben?'

'Ah,' I said. 'Actually, you're right. I did do that.'

'You wanker.'

I knew he wanted to hit me again. And kick me. He wanted to hurt me so much I could feel it coming off him in waves. But I also knew he wouldn't. He couldn't. He was so angry it frightened him more than it did me. I could understand how he felt, of course. I hadn't cheated on his sister – what I'd done was a thousand times worse. What I'd done, in his eyes at least, was piss all over our whole history, hers and mine, and shown with what little regard and total contempt I held her life and memory.

He must've really wanted to kill me. I couldn't say I blamed him.

'You wanker,' he said again, wiping away the tears that had suddenly welled up in his eyes.

Then he turned and walked away.

6

'I'm having an affair.'

I guess when you drive Death around for a living the more humdrum bombshells of daily existence, when they're dropped, lose their power to stun, surprise, or even, as in this case, produce so much as a hint of a lift of an eyebrow. In other words, my brother digested this rather startling revelation with all the animation of an Easter Island statue on being told it was quite windy again, before asking a question so dazzlingly brilliant it was days before I realised just how brilliant it was.

'Why?' Ray asked.

'What do you mean, why?' I asked him.

'What do you mean, what do you mean?' he replied. 'I mean, why are you having an affair?'

'Why?'

'Yes, why?'

I shrugged. 'Why does anyone have an affair?'

'I don't know,' he said. 'Why do they?'

'I don't know either,' I admitted.

'Do you love her?'

'Who?'

He rolled his eyes, a habit he developed early in life and continued to practise even after a lifetime of being told off for it by our mother. 'The girl you're having an affair with, stupid.'

'No.'

'No?'

'Well, maybe.'

'Maybe?'

'Well, yes, I guess.'

'You guess?'

'Well, I'm not sure, OK.'

He leaned back in his chair and carefully sucked his olive off its toothpick, before slowly grinding it to paste in his mouth. Ever since the peanut episode, he always treated small, potentially windpipe-blocking foodstuffs with the utmost respect. We were at Zanzibar's, a place where we often met for martinis, even though neither one of us particularly liked martinis. We did it, I guess, because we both wanted a bit of old-fashioned glamour in our lives, and it was more convenient than taking up ballroom dancing or wearing cravats.

'You haven't exactly given this a lot of thought, have you?' he asked me. 'What about Cassie?'

'What about her?' I said.

'Do you love her?'

'Of course.'

'You do?'

'Well, I guess I do.'

'You guess?'

'Well, no, then.'

'No?'

'Well, yes *and* no – I think.'

'You think?'

'Well, it's hard to know sometimes, isn't it? Do you love Zadie?'

'Yes.'

'Without a shadow of a doubt?'

'Without a shadow of a doubt.'

'Really?'

'Absolutely.'

'And how would you feel if she was, I don't know, suddenly blown to bits in a plane crash, for example?'

'Heartbroken.'

'You would?'

'Totally.'

'Really?'

'Of course.'

I was impressed. Ray's depth of feeling for his girl-friend had a genuine effect on me. I felt like a heartless freak in his presence.

'Would you ever cheat on her?' I asked.

He didn't reply straightaway, as most people prob-ably would, 'yes' or 'no' or 'depends' or even 'never say never', but thought about it for a full thirty seconds, as if the possibility had actually never entered his head before.

Then he just said, 'No,' but with such a matter-of-fact conviction I just knew he never would, the sap.

———

My other brother, Truman, has been happily married for years. In fact, Raymond and I owe him an eternal debt of gratitude for selflessly throwing himself on the ticking time bomb of our parents' expectations and actu-ally producing grandchildren. I'm sure they'd begun to take our combined childlessness personally, if only on a genetic level ('What, aren't our genes good enough to pass on?'). It really did take the pressure off, anyway.

Plus, he managed to produce pretty good ones, too. Not a Posh or Becks wannabe amongst them, and they only used bad language behind their parents' backs.

Some years before this act of sacrificial procreation, however, while bunny-hopping round Europe in a clapped-out old Kombi, he met, and fell in love with, a girl from Buffalo, New York.

Her name was Bunty.

Bunty from Buffalo.

When Sam – the girl he'd only just started going out with before embarking on this great adventure, but who'd nonetheless been patiently and excitedly counting down the days to his return – picked him up at the airport he told her it was over between them.

'I've fallen in love with an American,' he informed her.

He probably should have waited until they got home, as she crashed into the back of a bus. He spent the next six months in hospital in traction, but for once, being left-handed proved fortunate.

Not being content with a mere holiday romance, when the time had come for Bunty and Truman to return to the respective lands of their birth (she to Buffalo, he to Stoke), they promised to write. And while the impact with the back of the bus broke most of the major bones in my brother's body, it miraculously left his left arm relatively intact. Thus he was still able to fulfil his half of the promise.

And write they did.

Daily.

It was a truly beautiful, and at the same time stomach-churning, thing to have witnessed at an impressionable age. They wrote daily, passionately, single-mindedly even, for six months. And not once, during this entire period of feverish correspondence, did he mention the fact that he was laid up in a hospital bed with his various limbs suspended around and above him. He instead invented a whole other life and reported that instead.

It was far more interesting.

When Truman finally got out of hospital and resumed his normal life, he attempted to reproduce it on the page. However, it really didn't read all that well. It was, he had to admit, pretty humdrum stuff. It was really nothing much to write home about, much less Buffalo, so he went back to reporting from that other invented life which had proved so fruitful in the letter-writing department. The world of vintage sports car racing, Loch Ness exploration, and romantic, windswept, Cathy-and-Heathcliff-haunted moors which he'd created for himself. He was so pleased to get back there that he wrote off half a dozen lightning-quick zingers that had Bunty, a whole ocean away, so completely agog that she determined to waste no more time in joining him.

This news was to be the death knell of their relationship. Truman, by this time, could not allow a face-to-face meeting. It would mean exposure. Explanations. Sharing his reality with Bunty. He had no choice. He had to end it.

He killed himself off.

7

'I'm going to have a baby.'

'*WHAT*?'

'I didn't say I'm *having* a baby,' Cassie clarified. 'I said I'm *going* to have a baby. One day.'

I started breathing again.

'Jesus,' I said. 'You nearly gave me a heart attack.'

'Would it be that bad anyway?' she asked.

'No,' I told her, 'it'd be worse. Much, *much* worse. I am totally, *totally* unequipped to be a father. I'd stink. I'd worse than stink. I'd reek.'

'You'd be great. You'd make a great father.'

This is the great delusion.

What on earth is it that convinces otherwise completely rational human beings that they can somehow perceive another person's untapped, untested, not to mention non-existent paternal instincts and make such a completely and utterly unfounded pronouncement? What was Cassie basing this supposed fantastic fatherly ability on, anyway? Had I ever, in my entire life, in words or actions, given her any cause to think that I would be anything other than totally crap if suddenly presented with a child and all the odious responsibilities entailed therein? I was a lazy, infantile, dysfunctional, anti-social, pathologically selfish mid-thirties male, and not only that, but I revelled in it. When I said I'd stink at being a father I was in no way whatsoever being modest.

I would.

I just knew it.

But try telling that to a woman who's already got you pegged as father material.

———

My own father had three children by the time he was my age. He proposed to my mother on their very first date. She said no. He proposed again on their second date. Again she said no. This went on for some time. Eventually she said yes. My mother was twenty-five when they married, my father twenty-two. My mother's mother wasn't very happy about it. She was anti-marriage. After giving birth to twelve children this was perhaps understandable. She also wanted my mother to be a nun. My mother's father would also have liked to see her become a nun, as indeed would have her eleven brothers. Becoming a nun would definitely have been the popular choice.

She married my father instead.

As a result, I guess, of all the religious expectations, someone, or to be more exact, everyone, had neglected to explain such basic stuff as where babies came from and how you went about making them to my astonishingly innocent twenty-five-year-old mother-to-be. She didn't have a clue. Their wedding night, not surprisingly, was a bit of a fizzer. My father was barely able to convince her that such disgusting things even went on, much less convince her to participate in any of them. As it was he had to do it (convince her that is) through the bathroom door keyhole as she sat on the other side of the door on the edge of the bath and stared at herself in the mirror.

That night my mother's head was reeling as it lay on its pillow in the dark. Convent life had never seemed so attractive.

———

Things, however, eventually sorted themselves out, and the end product was us: my two brothers and me. My father was responsible for, counting my mother, four other human beings by the time he was thirty. Of course my mother bore the brunt of most of the actual child rearing, but the point is that my father, younger than I am now, had the kind of responsibilities half of which would crush me like a cream cake.

———

In my case, the whole question of having babies was, at least for a time, looking academic anyway. For months following a couple of failures in an area that of course I'd read was quite normal (on occasion) for nine out of ten, or seven out of twelve, or possibly twenty-three out of thirty-eight men to experience, I had been trying, unsuccessfully, to screw up enough courage to make a tiny, thirty-second phone call. I would call, and hang up. Call, and hang up. Finally, I managed to call, *not* hang up, and actually go through the motions of making an appointment with my local GP for the middle of the following week. I could, I reasoned, always cancel.

I didn't cancel, but I did agonise constantly until the

appointed time arrived, and then sat in the waiting room staring blankly at a *Women's Knitting Monthly* while continuing to agonise as frantically as possible in the short time left to me before I had to do what it was that was causing me all this agonising in the first place.

And then it was my turn.

'Benton Kirby?'

I looked up from my *Women's Knitting Monthly* with a studied, casual 'Who, me?' look, before casting one last, lingering glance back at my magazine as though I'd been interrupted halfway through the most engrossing article I'd ever clapped eyes on.

I put it down, stood up, and silently asked, 'Oh Lord, why the fuck didn't I cancel?'

'So! . . . What seems to be the problem?'

Doctors, like policeman and pop stars, always used to be older than me. It was the natural order of things. I will never, even if I live to be a hundred, stop being disconcerted when they're not.

'Problem?' I said innocently.

'I mean,' he smiled, 'what can we do for you today?'

'We?' My eyes involuntarily darted around the room, half expecting to spy a half-concealed assistant hiding under the examination table, perhaps taking notes.

'Figure of speech,' he said reassuringly. 'I mean me. What can I do for you today?'

'Nothing.'

'Nothing?'

'Actually, I'm feeling much better, thanks.'

'Really?'

'Absolutely.'

'Are you sure?'

'Totally. Couldn't be better.'

'My God!' he exclaimed. 'It's a miracle. Please tell all your friends. It'll do wonders for business.'

I felt like an idiot, but I couldn't, I simply could not tell this complete stranger, whom I'd known for all of a minute, my deepest, darkest secret, no matter how many times I'd actually rehearsed just those exact words. Red-hot pokers and thumbscrews couldn't have dragged them out of me. At least, they probably could have, but it seemed unlikely this young slip of an MD would resort to torture just to extract my embarrassing little problem.

And then this happened.

'Let me just say two words,' said my very own Doogie Howser, and then he said them. '*Well – done.*'

I stared at him blankly.

'I mean,' he explained, 'well done on taking the first step. I bet it's taken you weeks to even make this appointment, hasn't it?'

It was uncanny.

'Two months, actually.'

'And I bet you've been agonising about it ever since you did, right?'

'Right!'

'You'd be surprised how often I hear that.'

I couldn't believe it. I had never, in all my life, encountered anyone, much less a still-snotty-nosed doctor fresh out of medical school, who had been able to so easily and deftly put me at my ease. He had a bedside manner other doctors would slit a throat for. I could have kissed him, and I was still sitting there, quietly jubilant at how lucky I was to have managed to find such a warm, sensitive, intuitive GP just when I most needed one, when, disconcertingly, he added this:

'Well, if you'd just like to drop your trousers,' he said, 'we'll get started.'

'Sorry?' I said.

'Just drop your trousers.'

'You want to take a look at it?'

'It's the usual procedure.'

'Is it?'

'Certainly.'

So I dropped my trousers as instructed, and sat down again, semi-naked and completely embarrassed, my trousers and underwear around my ankles.

'This will probably be easier standing up,' he suggested.

I stood up obediently.

'Now if you'd care to lean against that wall with your legs slightly apart.'

As bemused as I was by the whole procedure, I still shuffled over to the indicated wall and did as instructed. I felt like I was in some American cop show, busted and waiting to be shaken down by the NYPD, only I'd inadvertently come out without my trousers and the hardboiled detectives were playing paper-scissors-stone to see who had to frisk me. I also, however, turned around and peered over my shoulder in time to see the doctor, alarmingly, slip on a single latex glove.

'Now you may experience just a moment's discomfort,' he informed me.

'Jesus!' I said. 'Why, what are you going to do?'

It was his turn to look bemused. 'What do you mean, what am I going to do?' he asked. 'I'm going to stick my finger up your back passage.'

'*What*? What for?'

'To check your prostate, of course.'

'But I don't want my prostate checked,' I told him.

'You don't?'

'No!'

'Oh.'

We both stood there.

'Are you sure?'

'Of course I'm sure,' I told him.

'Oh,' he said again. 'I thought you did.'

'Well, I don't,' I said, beginning to pull my trousers back up.

'Well, it seems a bit of a shame,' he said.

'What does?'

'It's just that you're already in the position, I've got the glove on, and besides,' he said, 'it's actually a very good idea to have it checked on a semi-regular basis, even at your age. Still,' he added, sighing heavily, 'if you'd rather we didn't.'

He looked so disappointed I felt sorry for the guy. If sticking his finger up my back passage was that important to him, it would be churlish of me not to comply. 'Oh, all right, then,' I said, undoing my trousers again and letting them fall to the floor. 'Go ahead.'

So he inserted a latexed digit, which, to my equal amazement and mortification, triggered an instantaneous and dramatic reaction in my heretofore-flaccid member. In other words, it produced the kind of raging hard-on any rutting bull would be proud of.

'You've got a nice healthy erection there,' he observed.

'Thanks,' I said, as naturally as I could under the circumstances.

'It's the prostate gland. It sometimes has that effect.'

'Does it?' I said.

'Well, everything feels just fine and dandy,' he said, slipping off the glove. 'So – oh, you can pull those up now – what was it you wanted to see me about after all?'

I got my trousers done up with difficulty.

'Oh that,' I said. 'False alarm.'

8

'I'm going to have a baby.'

'*WHAT*?'

'I take it you're not pleased?' Georgia asked me.

'*Pleased*?' I said. 'Jesus Christ, we're seventeen years old. Your parents are going to kill me – then *my* parents are going to kill me! Either way I'm dead!'

'I wouldn't worry about that. You're off the hook,' she told me.

'What do you mean I'm off the hook?' I asked her. 'I may not be overjoyed about it, but I'm not about to start pretending it's all your responsibility. I'm as responsible for this as you are. We're in this together.'

'It's nice to hear you say that, Ben, but I mean it about you being off the hook,' she said. 'It's not yours.'

I stared at her.

'I beg your pardon?' I said.

She said it again.

'Whose is it, then?' I said.

'Roger's.'

'*Roger's*?'

'I know.'

'Jesus Christ. What are you going to do?'

'What do you think?'

'Have you told him?'

'Of course I haven't told him.'

'Do you think you should?'

'Why? So we can draw up a shortlist of names?'

'If only the room hadn't started to spin none of this would have happened!' I railed uselessly.

'It's no big deal. Cindy Plangton's had two.'

'Babies?' I said, much surprised.

'Abortions,' said Georgia.

'Really?' I said. 'I didn't know that.'

'Well, it's not something she really wanted announced at assembly, you know.'

———

I'd known Cindy Plangton even longer than I'd known Georgia. We used to sit next to each other at kindergarten, and she was forever pushing my pencils off the desk. When I complained to my mother about this, she explained it this way: 'She pushes your pencils off the desk because she likes you.' I didn't get it, but accepted my mother's psychological analysis nonetheless, and duly informed Cindy Plangton the very next time she pushed my pencils off the desk that not only did she like me, quite likely love me, but most probably even wanted to kiss me, whereupon she stood up, stamped on my pencils where they lay on the floor, and politely asked to be moved to another desk.

———

To this day I still don't know whether my mother was right.

———

Cindy Plangton was also, incidentally, the first girl at our school to develop breasts, although this has absolutely no bearing on anything whatsoever as far as I know.

———

'Did it hurt?'
'I don't want to talk about it.'
'OK,' I said.

9

The effect of the doctor's latexed finger up my back passage was, as spectacular as it might have been, nothing compared to the effect of Cherry's finger up the same orifice. At the sight of the incredible transformation her eyes bulged and her jaw dropped. My penis had truly outdone itself. I felt like a rampaging stallion. I felt light in the head from loss of blood. I reached for a conveniently yet discreetly placed condom, tore it open, and attempted, as suavely as possible, to roll it over my – for want of a better description – engorged todger. This is the part you never see in movies. In Hollywood they go from clothed, to doing it. There's no messy fumbling about with condoms that don't seem to fit. It had been a long time since I'd actually used one, and I briefly wondered whether I'd bought extra small by mistake or whether my penis could have realised every man's dream and actually grown.

Either way, I knew I was losing points at an until now unheard-of rate on the suave-o-meter, especially when it shot off and gracefully sailed across the room. I was just in the process of trying to decide what would be more embarrassing, going over and retrieving it or getting out my standby and starting again, when Cherry suggested we probably wouldn't need it as it was her safe time of month (she may have been a virgin, but it didn't mean she hadn't read *Cosmo*). I could've kissed her. In fact,

I was just about to do that at the very least when I heard the sound of a uniquely shaped piece of metal being inserted into an equally unique metal slot.

As only two people to my certain knowledge had such a uniquely shaped piece of metal, one of them being me and the other being Cassie, this was very bad.

First of all, I froze.

Then I panicked.

I knew we had mere seconds before we were discovered. Mere seconds, five, maybe ten, before my whole life changed, was turned upside-down and inside-out, had, in all probability, the very stuffing ripped bodily out of it and then re-inserted in new and extremely uncomfortable ways.

'*Hide*!' I hissed. 'It's my *girlfriend*!'

But there was nowhere to hide, nor was there anywhere to run. That's the problem with urban life: no back doors. Of course she could've hidden in the built-in wardrobe, but she would have had to take out half the clothes first. That's another problem with urban life: never enough closet space.

I heard the door open. I heard her voice. It said: 'I'm home!' The simple words filled me with a white-hot fear, and I realised, in that famous moment of clarity we hear so much about, that my terror was born, not of fear of the moment, of discovery, but of the future, an unknown future which, if I could be sure of anything in this world, I could be sure wouldn't include Cassie. 'I'm home,' ironically, horribly, would be the last words I would ever hear her say before she hated my guts.

And that's when I saw them. One of the sliding wardrobe doors was open, and crammed into the top storage space was a number of plastic bin bags filled with hibernating winter clothes. I leapt off the bed, hauled one down, and emptied its contents out onto the floor in a frenzy. Then I stood there, stark naked, clutching the empty black bag while Cherry cowered in a far corner, equally naked, but striking the classic hands over tits and crotch pose.

She looked adorable. Like Botticelli's *Birth of Venus*, only crossed with a rabbit caught in an approaching lorry's blazing headlights.

And then, inexplicably, she started to giggle. Not being a particularly giggly person, and this in no way whatsoever being an even remotely giggly situation, this uncharacteristic and inopportunely-timed fit was obviously an unfortunate nervous reaction, and I could hardly blame her for that. Especially when I dropped my eyes in the direction of her gaze, to where my erection, my incredibly inappropriate erection – the very same erection, in fact, which had so recently filled me with delight and expectation, and in particular expectation of filling her with delight – was still bobbing up and down and rearing to go.

'So this is how it's going to end?' I thought to myself, suddenly clear-eyed and calm. I might continue to wrestle my soon-to-be wrecked relationship away from the rocks, but the sudden surge and swell of unforeseen events, I knew, had already scuppered me, and was any moment about to give me a jolly good drubbing into the bargain. My body, all jacked up on adrenalin, may not have realised it yet, but the rest of me was already more than resigned to being smashed to pieces, obliterated even beyond salvage, and so I could allow myself the curious luxury of a moment's objectivity. What that moment revealed was so ridiculous I felt like calling time out so we could all just stand back for a few minutes in order to fully appreciate just how sublimely ridiculous it really was, except I wasn't entirely convinced Cassie and Cherry would see things in quite the same way. In fact, I was entirely convinced they wouldn't.

'Well, so be it,' I said to myself, as I clutched my bin bag tighter, Cherry stifled another fit of terrified giggles, and Cassie – my lover, partner, and best friend – proceeded to open the bedroom door just as if she were expecting to find her life on the other side exactly as she'd left it mere hours before.

———

Sorry, Cassie.

10

About a minute and a half before my brother Ray started choking on a honey-roasted peanut we were standing at the bar watching my other brother, Truman, dirty-dancing with a very drunk, very attractive older woman whose very big, very angry husband would appear, alarmingly and unexpectedly, a minute and a half later.

'Do you think he's happy?' I asked Ray.

'Look at him. He's having a ball.'

'No, I mean do you think he's happy in general?'

'Ah!'

'Married. A couple of kids. Mortgage. Jesus!'

'Get used to it, buddy.'

'What the fuck am I doing, Ray? Can you tell me that? Just what the fuck am I doing?'

'You don't know?'

'Haven't got a clue.'

'Pre-wedding willies. Don't worry about it.'

'Really? Is that all you think it is?'

'Honestly?'

'Honestly.'

'No.'

'No?'

'You don't want to know what I think.'

'Yes I do.'

'No you don't.'

'Shit,' I said, staring into my drink. 'I think I'm on

the brink of making the biggest mistake of my life, but I don't know what the mistake is – getting married or not getting married.'

'Little brother,' he said, picking up a honey-roasted peanut, 'let me give you the best piece of advice you're ever going to get in this life.' He popped the peanut into his mouth, and in the time it took to travel through that tiny space, from hand to mouth, the very big, very angry husband of Truman's very drunk, very attractive dance partner appeared, a very nasty-looking sawn-off shotgun in his hands.

'You fucking whore!' he screamed. 'Prepare to die!'

Zadie, Ray's soon-to-be girlfriend, was a lesbian, or to be more precise, in the process of becoming an ex-lesbian. She had, only moments before, broken this news to her girlfriend, or again to be more precise, ex-girlfriend. Zadie had, in fact, never been with a man, but had recently found herself more and more attracted to them, and less and less attracted to women. This had come as quite a shock to her.

'I don't want to be straight,' she tried to explain to her now ex-girlfriend. 'It just happened.'

When the big angry husband with the sawn-off shotgun appeared just as my brother popped a honey-roasted peanut into his mouth and screamed, 'You fucking whore! Prepare to die!' Zadie, who had only moments before broken up with her now ex-girlfriend, leapt to her feet and smashed an empty bottle of Australian Chardonnay across the back of his head, thus almost certainly preventing the deaths of a number of innocent people, my brother amongst them.

Ray, meanwhile, had collapsed on to his knees, unable to breathe owing to the honey-roasted peanut which had chosen that precise moment to lodge in his windpipe. He was slowly turning blue.

'Oh Christ!' I screamed. 'Is anyone here a doctor?'

Zadie stepped forward.

'No,' she said, 'I'm a lawyer.' Then she grabbed my brother, her own soon-to-be boyfriend, from behind, wrapped her arms around his chest, and yanked with all her strength.

The peanut shot halfway across the room.

———

Thank you, Zadie.

11

It was my eyebrows I noticed first. Suddenly, somehow, I could've impaled flies on them. They were so long and spiky I had to start trimming them. And there was another thing. I couldn't stop playing with them: stroking them, gently pulling at them, twirling them even. I would find myself lying in bed doing it, staring at the ceiling, mind blank, and I mean completely blank, and then realise with a jolt that I'd been doing it for ten, fifteen, twenty minutes. And it wasn't only my eyebrows. I was sure my nose hair was lusher than it had been mere weeks before, and I was also sprouting odd little hairs out of the most unlikely places: my left biceps, a knuckle, even an until recently baby-smooth buttock. And I knew what was next. Truman had recently told me he'd found a grey pube, and he was only three years older than me.

———

I remember my first (pubic hair that is). It just seemed to shoot out overnight. I went to bed as bald as one of my own Action Men, and woke up with . . . well, with a hair. And then for a long time nothing else happened. I used to take a look every now and then during the day just to check on any progress. Once in class while taking such a surreptitious peek my teacher spotted me and called out, the bastard, 'Don't worry, Benton, I'm sure it's still there.' I resolved there and then to devote myself to becoming a black belt at karate just so that I could one day similarly embarrass him in front of the whole class by breaking his neck with a single karate chop.

———

Long before we had pubic hair to interest us, Truman and I once blew our eyebrows off experimenting with dropping lit matches down a narrow, evil-smelling ventilation pipe we'd recently discovered. We would light a match, drop it in, then peer in to see what would happen. Nothing did for the first dozen or so goes, and then it did. Post explosion, we were left temporarily deaf, singed, lucky not to have been blinded, and eyebrowless. For a while it was fun having no eyebrows, and we would both draw each other's on with marker pens, sometimes giving one another big bushy ones and other times wiggly ones or even a debonairly cocked one, but for some reason Truman's never grew back again. Once he was the only one without them, drawing them on wasn't so much fun any more, so we decided to make some falsies. Trimming a bit of hair off his fringe, we got hold of some double-sided sticky tape and stuck the individual hairs to it, by their ends, which was about as difficult as it sounds. Then we stuck them in place and I stood back to survey the results.

'Perfect!' I proclaimed.

'Are they even?'

'Is Steven?' I asked.

'Let's have a look then.'

He studied his new eyebrows in the mirror from

various angles, and ran through a lightning-quick repertoire of expressions, from surprise to anger to quizzical indifference, before pronouncing them even better than the originals.

'This is going to be great!' he said.

———

Why having false stick-on eyebrows was going to be great I have no idea, but I do know I cursed my luck that mine had ever grown back, and wished fervently that I, too, could have a pair of falsies stuck on with sticky tape.

———

He eventually had a pair of custom-made eyebrows specially designed, which really were indistinguishable from the real thing, and which he would have happily left on all the time except that our mother insisted he take them off at night.

'In case you swallow them,' she said.

So every night before he fell asleep, Tru would stick them on the wall above his bed where they would be waiting for him in the morning like a couple of pet caterpillars. Occasionally, he would forget to put them back on and would wander about feeling strangely naked until he or someone else in the family realised what was missing and they were duly reattached.

———

When he was older and the novelty of being the only

kid in his class, or school, or perhaps even on the planet with false eyebrows had pretty much worn off, which was admittedly quite a long time, these same eyebrows were to present him with, on a number of occasions, a very unusual dilemma, namely: at what stage of a relationship did he tell a girlfriend, or potential girlfriend, that his eyebrows were not all they appeared to be?

'Personally,' said Raymond, the first time the situation arose, 'I'd wait until I had her hooked. You don't want to reveal too much too soon.'

'So you don't think I should tell her?'

'Depends. Is she hooked?'

'Well, she let me touch her tits.'

'Inside or out?'

'Outside.'

'Then I'd wait.'

As a relatively little kid, listening in to this exchange, I couldn't help but marvel at this strange, semi-grown-up logic. It seemed so complicated. So complex. So *needlessly* complicated and complex. In other words, I thought they were missing the blindingly obvious.

'But why tell her at all?' I asked.

Ray looked at me in shock and surprise.

'By God, the sneaky little rat's right!' he cried, making me grin from ear to ear. 'Why tell her indeed? We're not talking lifetime commitment here, are we? You just want to have your evil, wicked way with her, right? She need never know.'

'But what if one fell off while we were – you know – doing it?' asked Tru, not entirely convinced.

'Use extra glue,' suggested Ray, 'and make it quick.'

12

Years later and not long after Georgia had broken her neck and frozen to death I went out for a while with a girl I met in a bookshop. I was in no way whatsoever looking to meet a girl in a bookshop, or anywhere else, but had, in fact, been merely idling my time away by reading the most amazing load of old codswallop I'd ever read and thinking, 'This is the most amazing load of old codswallop, and yet someone not only deemed fit to publish it, but I have no doubt there are actually people who will buy it, and read it, and then tell their friends to buy it and read it, and if their friends have too much sense to do either, those same people will buy it for them for a present and then write a stupid inscription in it so they can't even take it back or even palm it off on some other sucker, and anyway they'll have to read it eventually because their imbecilic friend will pester them until they do.'

Why I had taken such a vehement dislike to this particular book I don't know, but I was just about to slam it shut and make a huffing kind of noise designed to show my absolute and total disdain for both it and anyone stupid enough not to slam it shut with a huffing kind of noise when the person next to me, who would soon turn out to be my new girlfriend, said, obviously to me because there wasn't anyone else there stupid enough to be reading the same book, 'Wonderful, isn't it?'

———

When we left the bookshop we both went our own separate ways, but not before we had exchanged phone numbers and promised each other we'd call as soon as we'd finished the amazing load of old codswallop we'd just been gormless or gutless enough to hand over perfectly good money for.

She phoned the next day.

'Wonderful, wasn't it?' she said.

'Um.'

'I cried and cried and cried.'

'Oh, me too. Well, not actually cried, but I definitely got a bit misty once or twice.'

'What was your favourite part?'

'My favourite part? Well, there were so many. What was yours?'

'When she died.'

'That was your favourite part?'

'Then came back to life.'

'Oh yeah, that was nice. I like a happy ending.'

'And then she died again!'

Of course I should've stuck to my original plan of slamming it shut and making a huffing kind of noise, but when I had looked up to see what kind of total moron could have made such a totally moronic pronouncement, I was instantly distracted by something that quite drove all other thoughts, including snooty ones, clear from my suddenly dazzled mind.

What she lacked in literary discernment, she more than made up for with the most wonderfully astounding emerald-green eyes I had ever had the pleasure to be transfixed by.

———

Apart from the eyes, to be honest, she really wasn't that good-looking, or indeed interesting, but my God, those eyes were incredible! They were luminous! Radiant! Like two bottomless pools of iridescent loveliness! I just wanted to hold my nose and jump in, which I guess I did as soon as I didn't slam shut that amazing load of old codswallop with accompanying huffing noise, and said what it was I said instead, which was this:

'Unputdownable!'

———

It wasn't destined to be a long-term or particularly meaningful relationship, but it was interesting for certain similarities it shared with Truman's eyebrow dilemma. None of these similarities had anything at all to do with eyebrows, however. Rochelle had them, of course, and as far as I know they were her own, and as far as eyebrows go, they were nice. As far as girls went, she was nice too. As far as relationships go, however, it wasn't going to go far.

The said similarity with Truman's eyebrow dilemma was this:

Falsies.

Not those, but the very thing, rather, that had stopped me slamming that amazing load of old codswallop shut and making a huffing kind of noise in the first place.

She wore contacts.

———

The thing was, I was so obviously taken with them, and so lavish in my admiration of them, that she didn't like to disappoint me and admit that not only were they contacts, but that she had them in puce and indigo as well. So instead, once things had progressed to the going to bed with each other stage, she would lie awake until I had fallen asleep before taking them out and then wake up before I woke up so that she could put them back in again, which must have been exhausting.

How long she intended to carry on like this I don't know, but of course it was only a matter of time before the truth came out, which it finally did one day when, owing to a general fuzziness from lack of sleep, she wasn't paying attention to what she was doing and stepped off the kerb into the path of an oncoming car, breaking both her legs, one in three places.

———

I wasn't with Rochelle at the time of her accident, but raced to the hospital as soon as I heard, where I found her, bruised and battered, with legs pinned, plastered and suspended, sleeping peacefully, or at least bombed out of her brain. I sat beside her dutifully for an hour flicking through a magazine and was just about to go as an hour sitting in a hospital flicking through a magazine next to a girlfriend I wasn't even all that keen on was about as long as I could stand when she began to stir. I put the magazine down and was waiting for her to fully surface, with my 'Who's been a silly duffer?' or 'The car's asking for a re-match' at the ready, when she opened her eyes.

I instantly knew something was wrong, but I didn't know what.

What I did know was that I wasn't dazzled.

Or transfixed.

I didn't want to hold my nose and jump into those bottomless pools of iridescent loveliness (actually I was already over wanting to do that).

And then I realised, of course, what it was.

They weren't emerald green.

They weren't even green.

They were brown.

Nondescript brown.

Nondescript *mud* brown.

———

I didn't tell her it was over then and there, of course, although it would have been easier, what with her being heavily medicated at the time. I did the right thing and told her the next day.

'I don't care what colour your eyes are,' I said, 'it's the fact that you thought I would care. I don't think I can be with someone who thinks I'm that shallow.'

13

I don't know if most people check, but I do. And when I saw the souvlaki-sized turd still bobbing about in the bowl, I both cursed my luck and thanked my lucky stars for being so anal, then shivered at the thought of someone else, namely Cherry, coming in to powder her nose all aglow with the romantic possibilities of the evening and finding my little brown deposit. So, in one way it was a narrow escape, but there I still was, at an early, yet decidedly crucial stage of the relationship, having been invited round for dinner for the first time, and now, post dinner, finding myself in a second-flush scenario.

Of course the rational human being in me knew there was absolutely nothing to be embarrassed about. The rational human being in me, if left entirely to his own devices, also probably wouldn't wait, bladder bursting, for a free cubicle when a large, luxurious and barely attended trough went begging, or make a great show of rustling his newspaper violently every time he squeezed one out in order to cover any embarrassing plopping sounds, even in the privacy of his own bathroom. Nor would the rational human being in me feel it necessary to take a dump as quickly as was humanly possible in order that his Korean girlfriend-to-be sitting in the living room next door would think he was only taking a tinkle. But sadly, the rational human being in me is easily overridden.

Needless to say the not-taking-a-dump-but-a-leak

subterfuge was already up. Who needs to flush twice for a whiz, excepting, perhaps, the extremely incontinent (which wasn't exactly the impression I was trying to make either). No, I would simply have to bite the bullet, and flush again. I would just have to accept that she was under no illusions as to what I was doing in there, and not only that, but that whatever it was I was doing was taking some shifting.

And so I flushed.

And waited.

And watched.

———

'Fuck!'

A third flush was unthinkable, and time, now, was of the essence. I could dispose of it in the small flip-top bin beside the loo, but there would still be the risk – however slight – of its discovery. Something could accidentally fall into it, a lipstick or pair of tweezers; it could be knocked over, the bag could burst en route from the bathroom to wherever it was eventually disposed of. All unlikely, I'll admit, but possible, and all so unbearably embarrassing to contemplate that I almost instantly ruled it out in favour of dropping it out the bathroom window.

Unfortunately, I was foiled here by my inability to get it open more than half an inch, clearly not enough to dispose of what needed disposing of. And so, having wasted precious seconds, I was compelled to resort to my last, and most desperate measure. Scooping it out with the toilet brush, I wrapped it in a great wad of toilet paper, and gingerly slipped it into my trouser pocket.

———

Attributing the duration of my visit, insanely, to a sudden attack of leg cramp, and then explaining what leg cramp was, and how it was best got rid of, and then expounding on how and why I might have been struck down by such a thing in the first place, and that, while waiting for it to pass, I thought I might have absent-mindedly flushed the toilet a second time by mistake, I was so convincingly simple-minded that I'm sure she never guessed what had really gone on, even if she did begin to suspect I was an idiot.

Bouncing back, however, and as difficult as it was to be irresistibly romantic with my own turd in my pocket, I managed to such an extent that we were soon making out like a couple of teenagers. We kissed like two people who had just discovered kissing – or in my case, re-discovered it. But my ultimate goal of getting my trousers off before the inevitable squashage occurred wasn't achieved, even as I did achieve another goal: unhooking Cherry's bra. It may not have been done with any great aplomb, perhaps, but the great thing was it was done. Unfortunately I hadn't thought it out sufficiently before-hand and had secreted the offending item in the wrong pocket. That is, my right pocket when I was sitting on Cherry's left, which meant, basically, it was bound to come between us unless I managed to get my trousers off in time, which I didn't, although it had looked promising.

It was a very unpleasant sensation.

Actually, caught up in the heat of the moment as I was, it had amazingly managed to slip my mind, and so I was doubly horrified to be reminded at such a moment, especially when I caught the first, faint, yet unmistakable whiff.

I instinctively jerked away from her, which was in the opposite direction I think she was expecting. She looked at me in surprise and I stared back at her in confusion. Then, for want of anything remotely better to do, I grabbed my leg.

'Argh!' I groaned, clutching my calf in apparent agony. 'Cramp!'

'Again? Are you OK?' she asked, genuinely concerned and rearranging herself.

'*It'll – pass – in a – minute,*' I told her grimly through clenched teeth.

'Can I do something?'

'No, no – yes! Maybe a glass of water,' I said, smiling weakly.

As soon as she was gone I leaped up, crammed my feet into my shoes without untying the laces which I hadn't bothered undoing when I'd slipped them off at the start of what had promised, another lifetime ago, to be a night of sublime romance and quite possibly sex, and stood waiting ready to go by the time she re-appeared ten seconds later with the requested glass of water.

'Thanks,' I said, taking it and gulping it down with accompanying cartoonish gulping sounds.

'Are you going?'

'Well, it is getting late,' I said, handing the glass back and glancing at my watch. It wasn't quite eight o'clock. It wasn't even dark yet. 'School tomorrow, you know. We don't want to both be late, do we? People will begin to talk, ha ha ha,' I babbled, making for the door and all it represented: escape, freedom, an end to this night's humiliations, an end to this relationship, an end to my job even as I knew I would never be able to show my face there again, at least not until Cherry, and anyone Cherry might speak to, and anyone they might pass it on to by way of an amusing anecdote they'd once heard about one of their teachers, had left, not only the school, but preferably the country as well. Fumbling at the lock, I tore it open and almost leapt out the door. 'Thanks for dinner. It was delicious. Bye!'

———

When I got outside I found I'd inadvertently slipped the little party pooper into the same pocket as my keys.

———

Perfect.

14

At least I managed to get the bag over Cassie's head in one go. She screamed – naturally she screamed. If I had had time to think about it beforehand I would have expected screaming, but what I really wasn't expecting, what I probably wouldn't have expected even if I had had time to think about it, was the wild, uncontrollable flailing. Before I even had time to pull the yellow plastic drawstrings she had hurled herself violently away from me and crashed headlong into the mirrored door of the fitted wardrobe, which disintegrated in a shower of shards. From there she ricocheted on to the dressing table, sending its contents flying in all directions, before bouncing off that on to the bed, where she turned a somersault, careered off the side and with a wince-inducing thump cracked her head on the wall, thankfully knocking herself unconscious.

———

When I say thankfully knocking herself unconscious I mean thankfully knocking herself unconscious and not knocking herself dead, which is what we both at first thought she had obviously done.

'Oh my God!' said Cherry, and then, understandably, she said it again. 'Oh my God!'

She looked at me. I looked at her. We looked at poor

Cassie with her head in a green plastic bin bag and her legs in the air, feet propped up on the edge of the bed, concertinaed between it and the wall.

The next second I had leapt across the bed and was at her side. I pulled off the bin bag, fully expecting the back of her head to be a bloody, pulpy, flattened mass, but it wasn't. She even let out a tiny groan, which produced both a sudden wave of relief and a slightly – but only slightly – delayed wave of panic, lest she should have recovered sufficiently to open her eyes, take in the undeniably unexpected yet compromising scenario, make the admittedly fantastic mental leap required, and thus arrive at the impossibly obvious conclusion of what had just happened.

And then, knowing perfectly well that what I was about to do could not, except under the most unusual and drastic circumstances, and probably not even then, be deemed even remotely acceptable behaviour, I did it anyway, and stuck the plastic bag back over her head. Then, pulling it down over her shoulders and tying off the drawstrings, I made a breathing hole in the general vicinity of her mouth, and half lifted, half dragged her up on to the bed.

She was more or less unconscious, but capable of coming round any moment, which didn't give me much time to do whatever it was I was going to do, whatever that was.

'Watch her,' I whispered to Cherry, who was so stunned by the whole episode that she had totally forgotten her earlier modesty and stood there, equal parts naked and dumbstruck.

I raced into the kitchen thinking, 'Rope!'; then, 'String!'; then, triumphantly, 'Tape!' Worryingly remembering the torture scene from *Reservoir Dogs*, I ransacked drawers looking for gaffer tape, or at a pinch electrical tape, but all I could find was some old leftover Christmas Sellotape with little Santas on it. Returning to the bedroom I hastily started binding Cassie's wrists and ankles with it, while Cherry searched for her underwear.

'I can't find my pants,' she said, rummaging about on her hands and knees.

'Who's there?' asked Cassie suddenly, freezing us both to the spot. She tried to move, realised she couldn't, and instead of struggling, lay perfectly still. 'Is anyone there?'

With an exaggerated jerk of the head I indicated the doorway, and Cherry, as carefully as she could, reached about her for whatever items of clothing she could find. Then, clutching them tightly, she edged inch by inch towards the door. Hardly daring to breathe, I glanced about for my own jeans, pants and shirt, located them, tiptoed round to retrieve them, picked them up and made for the doorway as stealthily as humanly possible for someone choking down their own violently palpitating heart. And then, at the very threshold, I tipped a pocketful of change and keys all over the floor.

Cassie's previous self-control exploded in a burst of white-hot panic. She bucked and hurled herself about the bed like a trapped wild animal instinctively sure of its own doom without quite knowing what that doom was, where it would come from, or why. '*HEEEELL-LLLLP! HEEEELLLLLLP! HEEEELLLLLLP!*' she screamed, tossing her bin-bag-encased head from side to side, her whole body convulsing.

Cherry had already managed to pull on her clothes, and stood in the middle of the living room, ready to flee, but still rooted to the spot, whether through terror or loyalty I didn't know. What I did know was that I had two choices. I could stifle Cassie's screams, gag her, then get dressed and leave according to plan (such as it was), to reappear moments later having apparently just missed the intruder; or else I could let her wail away while I did all of the above excepting the stifling and gagging parts, but rather more quickly.

I let her wail away, through, I like to think, a reluctance to subject her to the further indignities of stifling and gagging, but really I was scared crapless, and didn't have the nerve to go back in there. So I threw on my clothes, thrust Cherry out the door and prayed no one would hear her cries of help and come gallantly and inconveniently running to the rescue before I could pretend to.

'I'll call you,' I told Cherry distractedly once we were outside.

'Don't forget my pants,' she said, before stumbling away, stunned, bewildered, panty-less but still intact.

It was only when she'd gone that I realised I'd left my keys lying on the bedroom floor along with my loose change, and was now, having idiotically closed the door behind me, locked out with my girlfriend bound and bagged inside, rapidly screaming herself hoarse.

———

Like Cher, if only I could turn back time.

15

Georgia looked good, all things considered. Of course I don't mean when she came out of the snow, blue, stiff as a post, with her neck at a funny angle, but later, at the funeral. We – or rather her parents – thought an open casket would be nice, and surprisingly it was. I'd seen her look better, obviously, but I'd also seen her look a lot worse.

But she still didn't look good enough for her mother.

'You'd think they'd have given her a bit of a smile, wouldn't you?' she whispered. 'She has a beautiful smile. Radiant it is.'

'Was,' corrected her father glumly.

'Was,' said her mother. 'And I'm not sure about that colour. Doesn't really suit her, does it? Not really her shade. Still – she looks lovely all the same, bless her!'

'Considering they gutted her like a fish, the butchers,' added her father, in the same glum tone.

———

It was true, too. They did. Gut her like a fish, I mean. Still, it was what she'd wanted, and it's nice – if a little weird – to know there are bits of her still out there doing someone some good.

'I'm going to donate my organs,' she'd just announced, apropos of nothing, one day.

'Are you crazy?' I asked her. 'Do you know how much we could get for them on the black market?'

'I'm serious,' she said, and she was. When she died she wanted all her organs, not just a few of the choicest ones, to be used to help people who needed them. 'What's the point of taking them with me? I'm not going to need them where I'm going. I want them to go where they can do some good.'

'Really?' I said. 'You're really going to become an organ donor?'

'I think it's the responsible thing to do.'

'I agree wholeheartedly,' I said, and I did. Being buried with all your organs is like being buried with your pockets stuffed full of cash, or winning lottery tickets, or undiscovered Beatles acetate recordings. When things like cash, and winning lottery tickets, and undiscovered Beatles acetate recordings (and organs) are in such high demand, it's just plain pigheaded to take them with you. 'But,' I couldn't help adding, as I thought, judiciously, 'have you given any thought to the possibility that you might be mistakenly pronounced dead, and before you even get the chance to wake up on a slab and say boo to some poor hapless trainee mortician who keels over with heart-failure on the spot, you've been sliced and diced and had your heart ripped out and stuck inside the first disgustingly rich businessman or washed-up old rock star who comes along with a hundred thousand pounds and a dodgy ticker? Have you given any thought to that?'

Sensible girl that she was, she hadn't. Instead she called me an idiot, kissed me, and carried on as before, just as if she intended to live forever.

I went round to Georgia's parents' place to discuss funeral arrangements. I would have been more than happy to leave everything up to them, but they wanted to include me, and I suppose if she had fallen off the ladder and broken her neck a week later it would have been all my responsibility, and I might have been inviting them round to my place instead, so I didn't mind chipping in with the odd suggestion to help out. Not that I had much to say on the subject. We had only just got through planning the wedding, and I was fresh out of ideas.

'I think an open casket would be nice, don't you?' asked her mother, and added, 'Help yourself to another Bakewell tart, Ben.'

'I prefer the country slices, myself,' said Georgia's father glumly.

'That's why I got the variety pack, dear. Two Bakewell tarts, two cherry tarts, and two country slices.'

'So what's happened to the other country slice?' he asked.

'I think I might've had that,' I said. 'Sorry.'

'That's all right, son. I'll have a cherry tart instead. They're not so bad.'

'Actually,' I said, getting back to business, 'I'm not sure an open casket would be that great an idea.'

'Why not, dear? I thought it would be nice for everyone to have one last look at her. Just to remember her by.'

'You do know, don't you,' I said, 'about the organ donation?'

'The what, sorry?' asked her mother.

'She was an organ donor. She donated everything. The lot. Heart, liver, kidn–'

I guess I could have broken it to them a little more gently, as her father, at the mention of kidneys (it turned out he'd had some fried for his breakfast) choked on his Bakewell tart and sprayed a mouthful of crumbs all over the rug. His wife immediately began thumping him on the back.

'Cough it up, dear! Cough it up!' she told him, and to me, 'Pour him some more tea, would you, love.'

'Does he take milk?' I asked.

'Just a dash.'

'Sugar?'

'Two,' she said, still thumping him on the back.

'And a half,' gasped her husband.

I added the sugar and stirred it quickly, and handed the cup and saucer to Georgia's mum, who fed her husband a sip. He immediately had another coughing fit and sprayed it all over me.

———

Ray had dropped me there, and was waiting outside in his cab. I jumped in the back and slumped in its seat, sapped by the ordeal. He turned round and said, 'Everything OK?'

'They didn't even know she was a donor,' I said. 'Mr C nearly choked on his cherry tart when I told them.'

'What happened to your shirt?'

'What? Oh, Mr C spat tea at me,' I said.

'Why?' Raymond asked.

'He didn't do it on purpose,' I told him. 'He was choking.'

'I thought you said he was choking on a cherry tart.'

'He was. Mrs C tried to wash it down with a cup of tea.'

'Bad idea. Tea's too hot. Can't get enough down to dislodge the blockage,' said Raymond.

'Well, obviously tea's too hot, but it was the only thing handy.'

'Wasn't there any milk?'

'Yes . . .'

'Well?'

'I put it in the tea,' I said.

'A man was choking and you stopped to put milk in his tea?'

'Well, it would've been really bloody hot without it, wouldn't it?'

———

When she suggested a photo, I thought she meant of the guests, which was unusual enough at a funeral, but not as unusual as what she actually meant, which was a photo of Georgia and me.

'Um,' I said.

'Just get in there a bit closer,' she suggested.

I edged a little closer, not uncomfortably, because uncomfortably didn't even come close to describing just how uncomfortable I felt at the thought of having my picture taken with a dead person, albeit one I would have shortly married if death hadn't intervened.

'I'm not sure this is entirely appropriate, is it?' I protested weakly.

'Why ever not?' asked her mother. 'You *were* engaged. Now just lean in a bit,' she directed, lining us up with her Instamatic. 'Oh, that's nice.' She popped her head out from behind it a moment. 'I don't suppose it would be possible to make her smile just a bit, do you? She's got such lovely teeth.'

'How do you propose we do that, then?' asked Mr C. 'Tell her a joke?'

'Well, I suppose it'll be lovely all the same. She looks so quiet and peaceful.'

'Of course she looks quiet and peaceful,' I wanted to shout at her. 'She's dead! Karked it! Expired! As they almost say in the sketch, this is an ex-daughter. And taking pictures of dead people, whether they're smiling or not, is, if you'll pardon the expression, totally fucking barmy, as are you, you crazy cow, I've always thought so, and this just bloody well confirms it, not that any confirmation was needed. You're barking! Out of your mind stark staring barking bonkers!'

'Say cheese!' she said.

'Cheese.'

———

Georgia's mother once gave her daughter this advice: 'Never, no matter what else you might do,' she said, 'touch a boy's testicles, because once you do there's no going back.'

16

Truman first met Bunty in Spain, on the Costa Brava. It was in a little local taverna popular with backpackers and Tru had ordered the speciality of the house, the imaginatively named Spanish Plate. When it came out it was indeed a plate, but a plate swimming with baked beans, and plonked unceremoniously in the middle, a set of enormous bull's balls.

Naturally, what with everyone being young, and drunk, and on holiday, and it being a plate of baked beans with a set of bull's balls in the middle of it, everyone there, staff included, thought it the funniest thing they'd ever seen, although Truman, who'd always been a bit squeamish when it came to things like eating testicles, really couldn't face it, and had to order something else.

'I don't care what I have,' he said, 'as long as it comes from above the waist.'

But Bunty, who was also there, and who was obviously less easily put off, and ready to sample all life had to offer, bull's balls included, spoke up from the next table. 'I'll have one of those,' she said, indicating Tru's Spanish Plate. 'Or do they only come in pairs?'

'Have mine,' Tru offered gallantly. 'I haven't touched them.'

Once introductions were made, and Bunty's table had joined Tru's table, and Bunty was just about to tuck into

Tru's balls, so to speak, Tru's friend, Cliff Morley, who he was travelling round Europe with in a battered old Kombi, and who would himself soon fall in love, with tragic consequences, ruffled his best friend's hair and announced, 'If you think they're big, you should get a load of his!'

———

It was true too. Truman did have exceptionally large testicles. Not freakishly large, or so big that he tripped over them or anything, but they were definitely bigger than your average set of nads. Mind you, he had a huge shlong too. If I thought mine wasn't going to fit the first time I saw where it was supposed to go, I don't know what he must've thought. Complete strangers would comment on it at urinals, saying things like, 'What do you use that for, pole vaulting?' and 'You could've gone from outside with that, son.'

The first time he tried to have sex he got through half the positions in the Kama Sutra just trying to get it in. Needless to say word soon spread, as did a remarkable number of girls who came to regard him as their very own Everest, the mightiest peak in the district, and one they just had to mount.

It was only a matter of time, therefore, before our notoriously lascivious English teacher, Miss Crump, got wind that Truman was packing serious pounds in the pants department, and proposed that he help her clean her dusters after class.

Judging by numerous independent accounts it would seem they'd never been so well cleaned, and the reason there were so many accounts was because, unbeknownst to Truman, and obviously Miss Crump, the whole thing had been an elaborate set-up. A half-whispered, 'My God, it's huge!' here, a breathless, 'I've never seen anything like it!' there, all surreptitiously intended for Miss Crump's ears, and the naughty pranksters knew her natural inclinations would take care of the rest. When the invitation to help clean her dusters came, word went round.

By the time Tru and Miss Crump staggered out of the stationery cupboard on jelly legs, the classroom, the doorway, the windows (it was ground-floor) and the corridor outside, were all jampacked with wickedly grinning students who erupted as one and gave them the greatest standing ovation the school had ever seen.

———

Truman's friend, Cliff Morley, fell in love with a Canadian girl he also met while travelling around Europe in a Kombi, but with, as I've said, quite tragic consequences. These were, basically, that he was killed shortly afterwards, and parts of him eaten, by a very large bear.

This obviously didn't happen while they were driving around Europe in a Kombi, but some time after it had blown up on the banks of the Danube, where they abandoned it, tossing its licence plates into the famously blue, but at the time murky-brown river.

While Truman returned home by train to break the news to his patiently waiting girlfriend that he had fallen in love with an American, Cliff hopped on the next plane to Canada, where his brand-new Canadian girlfriend, and a large hungry bear, awaited.

———

Truman couldn't attend the funeral of his partly devoured friend as he was in hospital in traction with most of his bones broken, but he couldn't help reflecting on how things really hadn't turned out the way the two of them had planned.

'Sometimes things go without a hitch,' he said, philosophically, 'and other times you get eaten by a wild animal.'

'Or,' I added, 'driven into the back of a bus.'

When Sam, his girlfriend, or rather now ex-girlfriend, first heard about Cliff Morley being eaten by a bear, she said this to Truman:

'Lucky you didn't fall for a Canadian.'

17

When Cassie and I got back from the club, about daylight, we were both still buzzing like Winnie-the-Pooh trying to pull a swiftie on some bees. We were feeling very good indeed, but in different ways. I put on some Tangerine Dream, although I have no idea why, or even why I have any Tangerine Dream records, and stretched out on the sofa to contemplate these two imponderables to their accompanying plinking and plonking. Cassie, meanwhile, not to put it too bluntly, was so hot she thought her nether regions were about to ignite, and wondered whether I might be interested in fanning the flames.

Rather ungraciously, I wasn't.

Sex, for some time now, had become something I was in the habit of avoiding, rather than initiating. Worryingly, I seemed to be growing out of it, like some people grow out of Fizz Wiz and the Goodies. Back in the eighties, at the height of those heady, halcyon, new romantic days, I remember Boy George creating something of a brouhaha when he said that when it came to sex, he preferred a nice cup of tea. Of course he was probably lying his hair extensions off, and indulging in all sorts of coke-fuelled floppy-fringed orgies, but now I was inclined to agree with him.

Also, for some time, whenever I did have sex, or even thought about having sex, I experienced the strangest, most disturbing hallucinations. Inexplicably, I would suddenly see Liza Minnelli, and not a young Liza Minnelli either, not *Cabaret*-era Liza Minnelli, which wouldn't have been too bad, but Liza Minnelli now.

(Cassie, incidentally, bears absolutely no resemblance whatsoever to Liza Minnelli, young or old. The hallucinations were inexplicable, and their origin remains undiscovered.)

Not to be thwarted in her carnal pleasures, however, Cassie disappeared into the bedroom and the next thing I heard was moaning, which soon grew so embarrassingly loud that I had to turn up Tangerine Dream. Whatever she was doing in there, she obviously wasn't thinking of Liza Minnelli, and when she finally came, our neighbours' estimation of my sexual prowess must have soared.

But she wasn't finished yet, and continued to come, twice, three times, four, five, again and again, and as she did, my hallucinations made the obvious next leap, and suddenly there she was, in my head, Liza Minnelli beating herself off.

———

Whether this had anything ultimately to do with my future extracurricular activities I don't know, although I did, some time later, and purely in the name of mental health, kill an idle half-hour in class imagining each female student in turn (well, the attractive ones) lying naked on my bed pleasuring themselves. To my intense relief (and considerable pleasure) none of them assumed even remotely Liza Minnelli characteristics, although one, a Venezuelan named Conchita, did burst into song.

Coincidentally or more probably not, Cherry, freshly arrived in the country, also happened to be in this particular class, and was thus subject to my increasingly heated, yet scientific, imaginings.

If I had been awarding points, she would have won hands down.

———

I remember exactly when I started fantasising about having sex with Cherry as opposed to fantasising about Cherry having sex with herself, although the two did segue into one another rather neatly. Having just spectacularly brought her to an amazingly explosive climax by her own hand (or hands, once I really got her worked up), I decided to skip the last couple of students in the name of continuity and introduce myself into the proceedings.

Arriving home after a typically backbreaking day teaching prepositions and seeing how many times I could use the word pineapple in a lesson before anyone commented, I stripped off en route to the shower and, stark naked, stepped into the bedroom. And there, chest still gently heaving from her recent exertions, lay, not terribly surprisingly, Cherry, sprawled naked on my bed where I hadn't long left her.

'Teacher!' she exclaimed, when she saw me. 'You're naked!'

'That makes two of us,' I replied suavely, before demanding what she was doing there.

'Don't you remember? You told me to come round and you'd help me with my articles.'

'I did?' I said, surprised at my own dedication. 'Well, it still doesn't explain why you're naked.

'Oh,' she said innocently, 'I got hot waiting for you.'

I admit the dialogue was pretty corny, but the sex was great.

18

Cherry's lips, perfect and luscious at any time, and now smeared with sticky, glistening ice lolly, almost begged to be kissed. We weren't, as it sounds, still in my little fantasy world, but on a school trip to Brighton and, having managed to lose the rest of the school, were sitting on the hard-pebbled beach eating ice lollies. I can't say that I had planned it that way, but the moment was, unquestionably, perfect. To be honest, I hadn't planned anything. I'm not even sure I intended anything. But at the same time I knew something – whatever it might be – was going to happen.

We both knew it.

I leaned in closer. I tried to look into her eyes, but was almost hypnotised by those lips. They seemed to fill my entire vision, like a Salvador Dali sofa in a very small bedsit. I'm sure she didn't, but I could have sworn she even licked them, underlining, italicising, and adding exclamation marks to the message I was already receiving loud and clear:

Kiss me! *Kiss me*!

My face inched closer. Wrenching my gaze free at the last moment, I glanced up at her eyes and saw them open very wide.

Then I kissed her.

Her reaction was not exactly what I had expected. In fact, it was the reaction of someone who, far from expecting to be kissed, had never even so much as fleetingly entertained the possibility, had never imagined, dreamed, considered, surmised or guessed such a thing could happen.

She was, in short, gobsmacked.

'What did you do?' she asked, rather superfluously I thought.

'I kissed you,' I told her.

'Why?'

It was an excellent question. 'I thought you wanted me to,' I said.

'No, I didn't.'

'Sorry,' I said. 'My mistake.'

It could have been left there, awkwardly, an embarrassing false start, never to be restarted again, except for a curious look in her eyes. They appeared to have been, both literally and metaphorically, opened. I could see through them her mind grappling with the profound seismic shifts of the preceding minute and arriving at the impossible conclusion that she had actually enjoyed it, had perhaps subconsciously even willed it, and wouldn't at all mind a repeat performance.

And so, getting my restart, I kissed her again.

19

Cherry had an ex-fiancé, too, although not ex as in dead. He was her first boyfriend – in fact, apart from me, her only boyfriend. They started going out when they were teenagers. When she was twenty-five she suddenly decided she'd had enough, not just of him, but of everything, and decided that the best thing to do was start again. And so that's what she did, and this is how she did it:

She fled.

She fled him, her family, her country and her old life, dramatically, but almost of necessity, on the very eve of their wedding. I say almost of necessity because it meant there would be no time to track her down and change her mind, especially as this was to have been no ordinary wedding. It was to have been the society wedding of the year. Her ex-fiancé was loaded. His family was even more loaded. Cherry's family was loaded too, but her ex-fiancé's family was in a different league altogether.

When she skipped out on him, she also skipped out on a lifetime of having and doing exactly whatever it was she wanted to have or do, and then some. It should all have been so perfect, and would have been except for a single fly in the ointment.

She wasn't in love with him.

She had always been very fond of him, and I'm not surprised. He sounded wonderful. And of course he doted on her. His whole family did. Everyone, in fact, was slavish in their devotion to her. Unbelievably, she hadn't even allowed him to hold her hand for the first two years they were together, and it was five years before she'd let herself be kissed, which must have been hell, glistening ice lollies or not. Not surprisingly, they never even got close to doing it. They were both too busy saving themselves for the big day that would now never arrive. He never even got to see her naked, poor bastard.

They were, by all accounts, a couple of preternatural innocents, a seemingly perfect couple destined for a perfect marriage, a perfect family, and a perfect life.

But it wasn't to be.

———

She didn't tell anyone. She just packed her bags and left. Her own family would only have tried to talk her out of it. Her fiancé, obviously, would only have tried to talk her out of it. Her friends would have told her she was crazy, then tried to talk her out of it. In Korean society in general, and her stratum of it in particular, what she was about to do was unthinkably shameful. Not only would her fiancé's family never forgive her, but her own family would never forgive her. Her friends might forgive her, but they'd still think she was crazy. And she was far from certain that her resolve was up to all of that.

And so, as I say, she packed her bags and left – economy class.

So paranoid was she about detection that for the first time in her life she didn't turn left, but right, as she boarded the plane that was shortly to take her to her new life. She reasoned no one would ever think to look for her in economy.

At dinner she asked to see a menu and was told, in a tone she had probably never heard before, that it was chicken or beef.

———

Considering she was with her one and only other boyfriend five years before she permitted any lip action, gobsmacked really wasn't that bad a reaction on a first try. And whatever her initial reservations, she took to kissing like a duck to water. We were soon kissing all over the place, geographically if not anatomically. We became a couple of kissing addicts. I couldn't see her lips without automatically puckering up. I would lapse into kissing reveries at the mere thought of them, only to suddenly realise my tongue was actually lolling, I can only imagine grotesquely, between parted lips, moving back and forth in slow, dreamy simulation of the real thing, which was embarrassing at any time, but especially so in class.

———

Like a duck to water, as useful a simile as it undoubtedly is, still doesn't come close to describing how Cherry, once we finally got round to doing it, took to doing it. Her whole body turned out to be one perfectly tuned erogenous zone. Even her elbows were sensitive. She would come almost before I was in the door, and then at intervals of about every minute and a half thereafter until I collapsed, a quivering, spent wreck. Krakatoa couldn't have been more volcanic.

But that wasn't all.

She soon started showing definite signs of adventurousness.

———

'Close your eyes,' she told me. I did as requested, and when I opened them again she was standing in front of me, stark naked. Of course I'd seen her stark naked before, just not this stark naked.

'Look,' she said. 'I've had a Brazil!'

———

I read her first sentence with not exactly shock, but definitely a certain discomfiture. It said: *Fuck me*.

'Is it correct?' she asked.

We were studying requests, and it was, if a little brusque, certainly that.

'We don't usually use the imperative in requests,' I told her, loud enough for the rest of the class to hear. 'It sounds too bossy, like an order.'

'So you don't like it?' she asked, all innocence, and I think I might have actually blushed. 'Is this better?'

I read the proffered sentence: *I'm sorry to bother you, but would you mind fucking me, please?*

———

As sexually hair-triggered as she was behind closed doors, however, take her outside, to the park, or the beach, or even outside the norm, a stationery cupboard, a classroom, my desk, or just about anywhere there was some element of discovery, of being caught in the act, and she became positively combustible. Slipping her finger up my back passage for an instant erection, she would take advantage of any opportunity, no matter how risky, in fact the riskier the better, and go off like a box of fireworks ignited by a stray spark.

I knew if my nerves didn't give in, it was only a matter of time before my knees, back and heart did.

But of course it wasn't all about sex.

20

'We shouldn't see each other any more,' she said.

We were in her bath, leaning back facing each other in a tangle of legs. Cherry's nipples, just poking above the water, looked like two tiny, dark pink islands, while her body, like a temporarily submerged, mysterious and infinitely inviting continent, lay stretched out, clearly visible even by candlelight, below.

I lifted up a foot and kissed it.

'Why not?' I asked.

'Because you still love your girlfriend,' she said.

'But I love you too,' I told her.

'So what?'

'So naturally I don't want to stop seeing you.'

'What can we do then?'

'I don't know,' I said.

'That's why I think we should break up.'

I couldn't say exactly when this had become a recurring theme, but it had. Weeks had turned into months, and months had turned into a full-blown relationship, with its own expectations and demands. And now we'd reached this impasse. What had at one time seemed a mere technicality (I already had a girlfriend) and an insignificant hurdle (breaking up with her), had turned, I wasn't sure when, into a solid brick wall (I still had a girlfriend and didn't appear to be any closer to breaking up with her).

'It'll be OK,' I told her, again, but I no longer really believed it. It was true I loved her. I was crazy about her. It was also true I wanted to be with her, but I'd also realised something else: I didn't *not* want to be with Cassie. For a while I had wanted to escape, completely, to throw off my shackles and, without wishing to compare life with Cassie in any way to life on Devil's Island, make a single, do-or-die leap, Papillon-like, to freedom. I'd wanted to start again, start everything anew, with Cherry. I would do new things, meet new people, visit new countries. I would be a new person.

And then, one day, one particular, specific moment in fact, something happened, and things were never quite the same again. It was strange. I felt time slow down, stop almost, but I knew even at the time it was an illusion, an aberration, that time, despite the scientific impossibility, was in reality speeding up, and not only speeding up but propelling me at speed towards some irrevocable future beyond my control. And in that strangely slowed-down, speeded-up moment I saw things with a sudden, disturbing clarity. I saw that in order to have Cherry, to be with her, I would have to give up everything else. And more importantly, in order to give Cherry what she wanted, I would have to take it away from Cassie. I would have to wrench our lives apart, past, present and future. Of course she would never forgive me. I would never see her again, and everything we'd been, and done together, would be poisoned, and die, and finally cease to exist. And I saw something else, too. As beautiful, as exciting, as unique as she was, I saw that Cherry wasn't enough. She

summed it up perfectly one day when she said, 'You're
so used to having both of us, you need two girlfriends
now.'

———

'Oh-oh,' she said.

'What's wrong?' I asked.

She jumped off the bed and came back with a hand
mirror, and showed me.

'Shit!' I said.

It was a hickey.

A big, fat, unmistakable, unmissable, unhideable
hickey.

'I'm really sorry.'

'Oh, shit!' I said again, still staring at it.

'I'm sorry.'

I recovered slightly, but only slightly. 'It's not your
fault,' I lied, trying to sound calmer, indifferent even,
but obviously failing badly.

'I didn't mean to.'

'Don't worry about it,' I told her, but still studying
it in the mirror, the horrible, malignant, tell-tale collection of burst blood vessels, while my mind raced: *What
am I going to do, what am I going to do?* I could feel
the panic beginning to build in me, to grow, to swell,
until I felt myself expanding under the pressure of it.
I thought I could actually feel my body physically
expanding. If I hadn't been naked I'm sure seams would
have begun to rip and buttons pop. I wondered how
much time I had to try to do something about it. But
at the same time I also felt bad for her. After all, we'd

just made love, sweet, beautiful, wonderfully unin-hibited love. If anything I should have been surprised at not being covered in love bites.

'I've got to go,' I said, perhaps a little too suddenly.

'Wait,' she asked. 'Just five minutes?'

'I can't,' I told her, already pulling on my jeans. 'I don't know when Cassie'll be back and I have to try to do something about – *this*.' I stabbed a finger, accus-ingly, at my own tell-tale neck.

I threw on the rest of my clothes then looked at her, sitting cross-legged on the bed, naked, anxiously clutching a pillow to herself, looking up at me with those huge, perfect, almond-shaped eyes. They were already beginning to brim with tears.

'It'll be OK,' I told her, trying to sound as reassuring as I could manage, which probably wasn't very, but I couldn't imagine how it would be. My mind wasn't reeling any more, it was numb. 'I've got to go.'

'Kiss me.'

I kissed her, but for the first time ever I didn't want to. Suddenly her room, her perfume, her body seemed to cling to me, suffocating me, drowning me. I had to escape. I needed air, I couldn't breathe. My one thought, horribly, was to get the hell away from there, and never go back.

And as I closed the door behind me, and stepped on to the street, the cold light of day reacted, hissing and spluttering, with my fevered brain. The romantic fog which I'd been happily blundering along in suddenly lifted, my mind cleared, and that's when time slowed down, stopped almost, and within that slow-motion blur I got a nice long look at things, and that's when I really panicked.

21

I felt like a giant red arrow accompanied me all the way home, bobbing up and down above my enormously obvious hickey, pointing it out to anyone blind enough not to have noticed it by themselves. I felt people staring at it as they went past, I felt them hurrying to catch up to get a glimpse of it, felt them coming out of shops and crossing over the road to take a look at it, and imagined them all thinking just the kinds of things I thought when I saw someone with a dirty great bite mark on their neck, which, apart from the obvious one that they'd recently probably had quite good sex, weren't particularly positive. Of course I'd had hickeys before, and even given them, and I'll admit they have their place, but that place was definitely not on *my* neck, not *this* decade.

When I got home I rang the buzzer before letting myself in, just in case Cassie had come home early. If she had answered I have no idea what I would have done. Probably turned and fled before faking my own death, or kidnapping at least. But she didn't, so I let myself in and made a beeline for the bathroom, where, upon inspection, things looked about as promising as they had looked for Lorne Greene when his office block collapsed in *Earthquake* (before Charlton Heston turned up), or for Shelley Winters making it out alive when the *Poseidon* turned turtle.

It was so absolutely positively real it was unreal, and if I hadn't suddenly, in a blinding flash of inspiration born of sheer total desperation, thought of what I was about to think of, I'm convinced I would have really done the only other remotely feasible thing that had the vaguest possibility of not resulting in total and utter disaster, which wasn't buying a polo-neck (they gave me an itchy neck, and I would have had to take it off eventually anyway), but simply to disappear.

Likewise if I had been clean-shaven, the next thing Cassie would have heard from me would have been written on the back of a postcard.

But I did think of it, and I hadn't shaved, and although I was horrified at the sheer thought of doing what it was I was about to do, I lathered up and did it anyway.

———

People kill themselves in all manner of interesting and mundane ways, and I know some even on occasion slash their own throats. And while it's an intriguing question as to why they might choose such a messy means of despatching themselves, it's how they do it beats me. I know they probably use something a little more suited to the job than a plastic disposable razor, but the nerve required must be phenomenal. And there's the question of technique, what might be called the 'removing old plaster dilemma': slow and steady, a little pain at a time, or all off in one go, with the accompanying short, sharp flash of intense pain. I would think the second method was the more popular for throats, although in the case of plasters, I usually favoured the first myself.

Cutting myself shaving for me is like falling off a bike for someone who can't ride a bike but insists on riding one anyway. And yet, let me try to cut myself intentionally, to nick, to graze, to shed blood in the name of peace, harmony and my own skinny, worthless neck, and my disposable lady Gillette might just as well have been a particularly soft feather duster. My face looked immaculate. Not so much as a missed bristle, or a scratch. As I ran my hand over it disbelievingly I could have been in a shaving commercial, apart from the fact I didn't look remotely like a Greek god and I had the hickey of all hickeys pulsating malignantly on the side of my now perfectly shaven neck.

'Shit!' I said, and then, because it seemed more than appropriate, I said it a few more times: '*Shit, shit, shit, shit*!' What I really needed was a razor that had seen some action. Something old, rusty and preferably notched, that had been used to within an inch of its user's life, or legs, and then left lying about on the edge of the bath until it was sitting in its own little rusty puddle.

But here luck was against me, so I had to make do with Cassie's pumice stone.

———

The great thing to remember about pumice stones is that volcanic material in general is not designed to be used on faces. If, knowing this, one should care to disregard it and apply said volcanic material to where it has no business being applied, then so be it. Just don't expect the results to be pretty.

91

By the time I was finished my hickey looked like a shark had made it, which, although not quite the desired effect, wasn't as bad as it sounds, as it was very unlikely that I was having an affair with one (a shark, that is), and therefore (so my reasoning went), no suspicions of hanky-panky would be aroused, and with a single leap (tumble and trip) I would be free.

———

'My God!' said Cassie, when she got home a couple of hours later, which gave me another couple of hours to deservedly stew in my own juices. 'What happened to your neck?'

'I had a bit of an accident shaving,' I said, 'and I think the blade might have been a bit dirty. I think it might be infected,' I added, pleased with the way my little infection embellishment sounded: it had a definite ring of authenticity to it, I thought.

'Why didn't you use your electric shaver?'

Oh, good question.

'Conked out again,' I said. 'I think I'll have to get a new one. Or else grow a beard. What do you think about the mountain-man look?'

'I think it's a great look,' she said, running a hand over my baby-bum-smooth cheek, 'if you live on a mountain, with a bear. But unless you particularly want to live on a mountain, with a bear, I think I'd get a new one if I were you.'

Bantering under pressure like this is demanding, nerve-racking stuff, and definitely not for the faint-hearted. 'Well, as attractive as I do find bears, I have heard disturbing rumours that they've been known to shit in the woods,' I bantered back, as best I could, 'which is a bit of a turn-off, to be honest.' The trick is not to force it, or overdo it, but to make it sound natural, no matter how many buckets of blood you're sweating.

She was examining my neck closely now, so closely I suddenly couldn't think of a single thing to say. If my life had depended on a bit of banter I couldn't have come up with it. I had nothing. All I could think of was how couldn't she recognise that horrible mess for what it was, a self-inflicted pumice stone mauling, a desperate, pathetic attempt to obliterate the damning evidence of my tawdry tryst? Surely, I thought, she couldn't possibly believe I'd really done it shaving. Frank Spencer shaving with a cheese grater on roller skates couldn't have done a more botched job. I held my breath and waited.

'It's quite nasty, isn't it?' she said, and then, what I'd subconsciously been waiting for: 'We'd better get something on that.'

The all-clear.

22

My mother and father still hold hands. Georgia once asked me not long before we were to be married if I thought we'd be like that when we were their age, and it gave me such a nasty jolt I almost got whiplash. Of course it shouldn't have, as we'd already been going out with each other longer than most marriages, and were engaged after all, but it suddenly seemed so inconceivable, being their age, two whole lifetimes behind us, that the question literally made my head spin. Did I think we would be like that when we were their age? My God, I'd thought, what a question, a whole lifetime pre-empted, telescoped into cosy companionship in our dotage, which isn't to imply my parents were in any way senile, but still, they were old, look at them, is that how she saw us, is that what she was looking forward to? I was suddenly horrified, appalled at the mere idea. I wanted to break it off on the spot, to smash our life together to pieces and stamp them into the ground, and then dance a jig on them, and blow a big fat raspberry at marriage as well, and all it represented, like growing old together, that slow, creeping paralysis of realisation that this is it, this is your bed and you're going to have to bloody well lie on it, and sooner or later die on it, too.

'Of course,' I said. 'Don't you?'

Funnily enough, Cassie asked me the exact same question years later, and although it didn't send my mind reeling in quite the same way as when Georgia had asked it, it still gave me a bit of a turn.

We'd only been going out five years.

———

Burt Bacharach, in his song 'Make It Easy On Yourself,' points out that breaking up is very hard to do, and he's right, even if in the song he's the dump*ee* and trying to make it as easy as possible for the dump*er*, and in fact takes the whole thing way too magnanimously, and really lets the two-timing hussy off the hook.

Phil Collins, on the other hand, so the possibly apocryphal story goes, broke up with his wife, now ex-wife, or possibly ex-ex-wife, by fax. I don't know if this is true or not, but even if it is, it could have been worse. He could have sent her a postcard from somewhere nice and sunny, like Fiji, with 'Having a wonderful time, glad you're not here. PS I want a divorce' scrawled on the back.

Breaking up, of course, *is* difficult, or rather, breaking up with someone you still like, or even worse, still love, is difficult. Breaking up with someone in traction and heavily medicated whom you not only don't particularly like any more, but never particularly liked, is a doddle compared to that. And I imagine breaking up with someone whom you can't actually stand is easier again, and possibly even fun.

Breaking up with Cassie, whom I still liked, and loved, and who still liked and loved me, was not a doddle.

In fact, it was so definitely not a doddle that I didn't do it.

It was easier not to.

I thought, instead, I would let things run their course.

It's amazing what some people can convince some other people to do, and not just stupid people either, but all kinds of people, from all walks of life, who really should know better. Hitler convinced most of Germany that he was not only the bee's knees, the best thing since sliced bread and just what the doctor ordered all rolled into one, but that a war with the rest of the world was actually a pretty good idea, and managed to do it all while sporting possibly history's silliest moustache. Eve, if you believe that sort of thing, convinced Adam to do exactly the one thing he'd been strictly forbidden to do – by *God*, no less – and eat, as mind-blowingly tempting as it must have been, a piece of fruit, and not even anything particularly exotic, like a nice ripe mango, or a pomegranate, but a common-or-garden-of-Eden-variety apple.

But perhaps the most spectacular acts of dodgy persuasion are performed by ourselves, on ourselves.

I managed to convince myself that by not breaking up with Cassie, by fax, postcard or otherwise, and so sparing her the usual accompanying heartbreak and anguish, while at the same time continuing to screw Cherry every opportunity I got (and promising – and believing my own promises – her the world), I was in fact not being the total cowardly bastard that I was, but, rather, the unhappy victim of my own selflessness and overdeveloped conscience.

In other words, I managed to convince myself I was doing everybody a favour.

When I tried to explain this to Ray he told me to write it all down as clearly and precisely as I could, then to take the piece of paper, or more probably pieces of paper, and tear it, or them, into tiny little bits, and then toss the tiny little bits up in the air, and then, finally, to reassemble them again at random, preferably with my eyes closed.

'What for?' I asked him.

'It might make more sense,' he said.

———

Although I can now admit to being a total cowardly bastard, to be honest, I didn't really start feeling bad about things until I realised that I didn't actually want to break up with Cassie after all. Of course I didn't want to break up with Cherry either. Subsequently, even I now found it rather uphill work persuading myself I was acting any other way than abominably to very, very abominably. And when I say I didn't really start feeling bad about things until I realised this, I'm using the word loosely enough so as to be almost unrecognisable to most people.

The truth is, I didn't really feel bad at all.

———

This, as it had years before, worried me, which had the curious result of me eventually feeling worse about not feeling worse than about what it was I wasn't feeling bad enough about in the first place.

23

At the other end of the feeling-bad scale, of course, was Jamie. Years before, he'd advised me not to worry about not feeling worse about Georgia falling off a ladder and breaking her neck and freezing to death, but that was easy for him to say. He gave up an extremely unpromising career as a cabaret entertainer (unpromising because he couldn't sing, dance, or even mime, and platforms gave him vertigo) for an even more unpromising one working as a carer in the most sordid, squalid and generally soul-crushing nursing home he could get a job in, which wasn't difficult as they would have hired just about anyone who was willing to work there, so sordid, squalid and soul-crushing was it.

'Don't ever,' he told me, after only his first day on the job, 'put – or let anyone else put – your parents in a nursing home. Do them a favour and put a bullet in their brains first.'

He didn't need to work in a nursing home, of course, and he definitely didn't need to go out of his way to find the worst one he could. He was young and flamboyant, with a large collection of feather boas besides. He could have done anything he wanted, short of singing, dancing, miming or wearing high heels for a living.

'You're crazy,' I told him, when he first told me.

'Maybe,' he said.

'There's no maybe about it. You do realise you'll be

changing nappies. Old people nappies,' I added, with emphasis.

'Someone has to,' he said simply.

'Someone has to eat dog food to test it's not too disgusting even for dogs to eat too, but you don't see me rushing my résumé off to Pal, do you? In this society there are just certain jobs that we must assume are being done by people other than us, so that we can get on with not thinking about them, and testing dog food for yumminess and checking old people's pants for parcels are most definitely two of them.'

'I'm doing it for Mum.'

Of course I knew why he was doing it. It was obvious why he was doing it. He was trying to make amends. He was doing penance. He was racked with guilt, not for putting his dear old Mum in a nursing home, but for killing her, or as good as killing her as far as he was concerned. He just wanted to make it up to her, somehow. Of course I knew all this, I just thought it was a bloody lunatic idea.

But I was wrong, even though I could never have done what he did, or, for that matter, feel the need to.

Whether changing nappies, or giving sponge baths, or just treating his patients like ordinary human beings, Jamie became a force of good, not in any major, ground-breaking, or look-at-me way, but in a small, day-to-day, seemingly insignificant way that nonetheless gave a bunch of people a bit of dignity back for a little while before they finally popped their carpet slippers.

———

Of course I wasn't totally devoid of feelings. I wasn't a monster, or anything. I felt bad about a lot of things. Our murdered goldfish, for instance. I found them early one morning, a dozen or so tiny orange squishes around the edge of their pond.

'Why would anybody want to squash our goldfish?' I asked my mother tearfully, who told me there were some people who just hated anything that was beautiful. 'So if we had ugly fish they wouldn't squash them?'

'Well, then they might squash them because they were ugly,' she said, and then to confuse me even further, added, 'Or because they didn't like fish. Or because you had fish, beautiful, ugly or otherwise, and they didn't. Or because they had nothing better to do, or even because they just felt like squashing something.'

So terrifyingly bleak a picture did she paint of the chances of a fish surviving the vicious vicissitudes of this world that I swore I would never have another one.

24

Two days after Fiona told me I should try using an electric razor she had a nervous breakdown and started throwing marker pens at her students, screaming, 'Speak English, God damn you, it's not that fucking hard!' Unfortunately it was, as she was teaching a beginners' class at the time.

But she wasn't the only teacher I'd known to flip.

Reg Diplock was another one.

After a number of complaints from students that they weren't learning anything in his lessons, a common enough gripe in general, our Director of Studies asked him if he would mind if she sat in on one. He said he wouldn't mind at all, in fact he would be delighted. So she set herself up unobtrusively at the back of the class while Reg took his place at the front, behind his desk. While the students waited, not terribly expectantly, having a pretty good idea what was to come, or rather wasn't, Reg proceeded to take out a book – *What Katy Did Next*, having got through *What Katy Did* the week before – and, silently, started to read.

After five minutes sitting there in a silence only punctuated by the occasional nervous fidget or turning of a page, waiting for something else to happen, our DoS leaned over to the nearest student, and asked, 'Is this it?'

Apparently it was.

'Can I see you outside for a minute, Reg?' she said.

Outside, before she could say anything, he asked her how she was enjoying the lesson.

'Sorry, Reg,' she said, 'are you taking the piss?'

'You're not enjoying it then?' he asked, genuinely surprised.

'Enjoying what exactly, Reg? You're sitting there reading a bloody book, for God's sake.'

'Oh, I see what's happened,' he said. 'You've had caffeine this morning, haven't you? Caffeine always interferes with reception. My students know not to drink it. My fault. I should've warned you.'

What the caffeine was interfering with, apparently, was the reception of the lesson Reg was telepathically transmitting to his caffeine-free students. Apart from being a vastly superior way of imparting and absorbing knowledge, it also enabled him to catch up on his reading, though his choice of reading material was less easily explained.

He had learned the technique from the dolphins while swimming off Byron Bay, Australia, and could also summon UFOs, which he may well have done to get home after being escorted from the premises and asked never to set foot on them again.

'If you could be anything in the world, Tomoko,' I asked her, reviewing her grasp of the second conditional, 'what would you be?'

She thought about it very carefully before answering, as if she thought there might be some chance of me actually being able to grant it.

'I will be man.'

'Would.'

'I would be man.'

This was a pretty common answer, for female students at least. Male students, already being men, I guess, usually opted for rich, although I did have one Thai student who said he would be a woman, and indeed soon after became one.

'Why?' I asked her.

She didn't have to think about this at all.

'Because then I can be bus driver.'

25

At least the world needs bus drivers, and at least Tomoko knew what she wanted to be. I, on the other hand, had not only never wanted to be a bus driver, but I'd never wanted to be a fireman, or a lumberjack, or an astronaut, either. In fact, I'd never really wanted to be anything in particular. I was virtually ambitionless. Virtually, because I wouldn't have actually minded being Dr Who, what with all the travel and crumpet, but I'd never set my hopes on it or anything. I would have had my Careers Adviser at school pulling her hair out except she didn't have any. So, when finally faced with the seemingly infinite possibilities which higher education offered, the first thing I did was narrow the choice down by deciding I would study something ending in Y. This still left me with quite a choice on my hands – anthropology, archaeology, psychology, philosophy, and theology, just to name the first five that popped into my head (I stopped at five for simplicity's sake, but substituted astronomy for theology, hoping God wouldn't take it personally).

I wrote down each word, then stared at them in turn, hoping one of them might suddenly ignite some hitherto dormant spark of interest, but none did. They might all just as well have been synonyms for blancmange. Of course I could've just chosen five different subjects, perhaps ending in G this time, but G subjects all sounded so solid and practical (engineering, computing, and worst of all, accounting). Besides, now that I'd come this far, I was reluctant to start all over again. So instead I found the most readily available picture representing (or at least approximating) each subject – a monkey, Harrison Ford, a couch, Rodin's *Thinker*, and ET (of course I'd wanted one of Galileo) – and stuck them on a dartboard.

—

I missed the board entirely my first two attempts, but not by yards, which wasn't bad for someone with their eyes closed, and actually landed exactly between the monkey and Harrison Ford on my third. I was tempted to just call it archaeology, and let it go at that, but it seemed a little arbitrary somehow, so I had another shot and hit *The Thinker* right in the backside.

—

I once wrote a paper on Sartre and how, although his philosophy was pretty gloomy (not to mention his titles: *Being & Nothingness, No Exit* and *Nausea*, anyone?), and he wasn't very good-looking (he was no young Schopenhauer, for example), he was by far and away the most successful philosopher with girls.

—

By the time I went away to university I myself had been successful with the grand total of one girl. Partly for this reason Georgia and I both thought it would be a good test of our relationship if we went to different universities, in different cities, and I guess it was, although in all likelihood if we had gone to the same one the chances are we probably would have eventually broken up, or at least not planned to marry so soon, and so she wouldn't have been trying to climb through that unlocked upstairs window after losing her keys on her hen night and slipped and broken her neck, and would still be alive today, but then again, who knows? She might just as easily have been hit by a bus driven by a Japanese woman who'd had to go to all the trouble of emigrating just in order to fulfil her lifelong dream of one day being a bus driver, or else have choked to death on an alfalfa sprout (it happens, apparently).

———

Not long after we had both graduated, and Georgia had rather decisively ruled out any post-graduate studies by breaking her neck and freezing to death, I realised that a philosophy degree and a dead fiancée had more in common than I would have imagined before I had one of each, namely: they're not particularly good for anything, they don't make for decent small talk, and they're not much help in picking up girls.

———

After four years grappling with many of the most difficult and obscure concepts ever dreamed up, expressed in prose so convoluted and unwieldy that deciphering it was like rolling a small boulder uphill, along a goat track, at night, while balancing a pencil on your nose, I also arrived at the conclusion that there were only two questions in the entire history of asking questions that were really worth asking, and both of these, as far as I could make out, were unanswerable.

How? and *Why?*

26

Having just spent four years doing something based on a decision based on throwing a dart at a dartboard with my eyes closed based on another decision to study something ending in Y which was based on nothing whatsoever, I decided, when I saw the advertisement for a recruitment night for summer temps at Madame Tussaud's famous Waxworks to go along, based more on an idle curiosity in seeing Kylie Minogue, it must be said, than on any particular desire for gainful employment. As it turned out I managed both, as well as making the startling discovery that Kylie (or at least her wax doppelgänger) was nipple-less (although Grace Jones was not).

———

People would queue for hours to get into the place, then they'd shuffle around saying things like, 'Who's that?' and 'He's shorter than I imagined' and 'How come Kylie doesn't have nipples?' (or at least they would have if they had only known). Sometimes they would prod you to see if you were real, or so that they could make a joke, which was always the same one. 'Just checking,' they'd say, at which point you'd smile wearily and fantasise about how satisfying it would be just to knee them in the goolies. Sometimes people would cop a quick, surreptitious feel (usually of the models, but of the guides as well if they were lucky). Linford Christie was particularly popular with the ladies, while it was a full-time job keeping randy fans off the diminutive Ms Minogue, nipple-less though she was (a situation which wasn't improved when they updated her model with one of her conveniently positioned on all fours).

———

'What do you do with all the old dummies?' an elderly American visitor once asked me. 'You know, when they're not so famous any more?'

'We melt them down and make them into candles,' I told him.

'Is that a fact?' he said. 'Do you think I'd be able to buy me a couple of that Napoleon? Or if he's all gone, maybe that Henry the Eighth fella. You should have been able to make a good few candles out of him.'

———

I once had a conversation with Candice Bergen too. It went like this:

'How do I get in?' she said, rather brusquely I thought.

'Well, this is the exit,' I told her, with just a hint of retaliatory snootiness, 'so not this way.'

'So where do I go?'

'The entrance,' I suggested.

'Where's that?'

'At the front of the building.'

'Where am I now?'

'At the back of the building.'

'This whole goddamned country is back to front if you ask me,' she said, and disappeared the way she had come in, which was through a large door with lots of people leaving through it marked EXIT.

———

Michael Jackson was another famous visitor, but outside usual opening hours. This visit was conducted with all the precision of a major military operation, and we (the staff) were under strict orders to speak only if spoken to, and under no circumstances whatsoever tell Michael he was bad.

27

I'd only ever intended it as a stopgap, a kind of holding station between my old and new lives. The one was now behind me, dead and buried, literally, while the other, hovering somewhere on the horizon, was as fuzzy and unfocused as a bad foreign film (that is, plotless, inscrutable, and more than a little daunting). If life really is a journey, I was about as ready to set out on the next stage of mine as the Incas had been ready for the Spanish pox. My shoes pinched, I was wearing entirely the wrong kind of clothes, and my compass was a piece of crap. It could point North all right, but it couldn't tell me which direction I was supposed to go.

Madame Tussaud's, however, was soon to prove to have its own strangely irresistible gravitational force, capable, it seemed, of trapping and holding the less directionally motivated amongst us in a listless, enervating and potentially permanent orbit. People had grown old working there. People had grown old and died working there. People had even, I could have sworn, grown old and died and continued working there. Of course, I stayed for the uniform (chicks dig museum attendants in one-size-fits-all blazers and soup-stained ties) and for the staff canteen repartee.

'Does that sausage look familiar to you, Larry?' asked Vern, an irrepressible cockney comic genius who should have had his own TV show with regular guest spots on

Parky, but instead spent his life nervously sitting on the toilet during Spurs matches and cracking endless jokes, usually at the expense of his dour and possibly psychotic friend, a Canadian expat named Larry, while at work.

'Whatever,' replied Larry.

'I love this man, Maria,' Vern told the large, grinning woman doling out almost recognisable food from the other side of the counter. 'I really do. And what's more, I respect him. I do, Larry. I love and respect you as a human being. It's not your fault you're a complete failure. I think your parents were very irresponsible. Everyone knows lumberjacks shouldn't reproduce with one another.'

'Are you going to order or what?' the long-suffering Larry asked him.

'I'm still trying to decide whether I feel lucky. Blimey, what's that?' he asked, pointing.

'That's bacon, darlin',' Maria told him, grinning broadly.

'Bleedin' hell!' said Vern. 'You mean it was bacon. It's more archaeological artefact than breakfast now. It looks like someone's leftovers from Pompeii. If I bit that me teeth'd snap off!'

———

I joined the two of them at a table with Frank, another lifer, as anyone who'd been there for more than a couple of years was known. Frank had been there for more like twenty, while Vern and Larry both tended to brush the subject aside whenever it arose. Frank was busy ploughing his way through an enormous fried breakfast. Vern watched him for a few moments with a mixture of admiration, wonder and revulsion on his face.

'Doesn't your missus feed you or something, Frank?' he asked at last. 'If I ate that much food I'd buckle at the knees.'

'What? My missus cook?' said Frank morosely. 'You'd have to be joking. She wouldn't cook a dinner in an iron lung. She doesn't get out of bed until midday, then all she does is sit around all day in her dressing gown and curlers, waiting for me to come home so she can tell me what a pathetic loser I am and how she's wasted her life on me. I think I hate her more than any other person I've ever known, living or dead.'

'Well, that's nice, Frank,' said Vern. 'It's always heartening to hear that marriage can still be a worthwhile and rewarding experience. So tell us, young Benton,' he said, turning to me, 'any plans to tie the old matrimonial slipknot youself?'

'Why would he?' asked Frank, before I could answer. 'He's probably got birds up to the eyeballs. Probably shagging himself silly every night with a different one. They're all at it, you know. Can't get enough.'

'Whatever you do, Ben, don't tell him it isn't true,' Vern told me. 'It's the only thing that's sustained him all these years.'

Larry suddenly banged his fist down on the table, making Frank and me – but not Vern – jump.

'Why is Maria always so damn nice to you, Vern, and so goddamn hostile to me?' he demanded. 'Can you tell me that?'

He had obviously been brooding about it since being served, although with Larry it was hard to tell when he wasn't brooding, as he generally was, and when he wasn't, he looked like he was anyway.

'It's my cockney charm, old cock.'

'Hasn't she ever heard of Canadian charm?'

'Who has?'

'Not a bad breakfast this morning, Larry,' said Frank, still shovelling his food away.

'Well, it's edible,' said Larry, still brooding, or possibly not.

'Only if you've got a stomach made of cast iron,' said Vern, picking a piece of bacon off Larry's plate and shattering it against the edge of the table. 'Do you think bacon's supposed to do that? That ain't crisp, mate, it's bleedin' fossilised.'

'Do you mind,' said Larry. 'I was going to eat that.'

'Then I might just possibly have saved yer life,' Vern told him, taking a sip of ever-present tea, 'if not yer bacon.'

Larry was a nice guy, but he was also a human keg of dynamite just waiting to explode. Something, although no one knew exactly what, had lit his fuse years before, and now it was no longer a matter of if, but when he went *boom*! After I'd once watched him punch out his locker in our changing room, I asked him if he was all right.

'Sure,' he said. 'I just felt a little uptight.'

'About what?'

'Everything,' he replied.

'You want to know about Larry? What's been eating him all these years?' Vern asked me one day. 'Well, I'll tell you. Larry here,' he said, placing a consoling hand on the other's shoulder, 'was the fifth Beatle. I'm not joking, man. They sacked him just before they made it big because he had unnaturally hairy forearms, he couldn't play an instrument, and he was Canadian, but not necessarily in that order.'

Vern ribbed him mercilessly, and I believe it was the only thing that stopped him from really losing it one day, and not getting it back again.

———

Vern, although without doubt the single most likeable person I've ever met in my life, was not quite universally loved. There was at least one person who was impervious to his charm.

'Look out,' said Frank suddenly.

We all looked up to see Sprigett, one of the exhibition managers, and a pompous little twerp of the first order, sauntering self-importantly towards us. For some reason he always reminded me of a pencil stub that had been over-sharpened to within an inch of its life, and he took great pride in an oversized bunch of keys which he wore, at all times, jangling from his belt.

'I thought I could hear goose stepping,' said Vern, 'and lo and behold, in walks one.'

He walked right up to our table, and stopped. He didn't say a word, but cast a withering glance over us before punching his arm out in that way that certain pompous little twerps do when they want to look at their watch. He even did it when he was wearing short sleeves.

'Well, gentlemen,' he said, studying his watch as if he were counting down the seconds, which he probably was, 'by my calculations your break has exactly . . . *one* minute to go. That's sixty seconds.'

'Is that a fact?' said Vern, leaning back expansively. 'Just enough time for another cuppa tea, then . . . Larry, get the teas in, pal. Me leg's gone all funny again.'

Sprigett curled half a lip at him. 'Cute,' he said, turned on his heel (literally), and marched janglingly out again.

'Silly pillock,' said Vern.

'For once I agree with you,' said Larry.

'That's nice, Larry, 'cause I was talkin' about you. And where's my cuppa tea?'

'I'd give a lot to see him get his,' said Frank.

'Perhaps we could take up a collection and pay Larry to assassinate him. What do you charge nowadays, Larry? Still two-pound-fifty?'

'I'd do it for free,' said Larry darkly. 'I even know how I'd do it. I'd get away with it, too. I've given it a lot of thought.'

'Oh, my Gawd,' said Vern, 'it's the Canadian Mafioso. Next thing we know a moose head'll be turning up in his bed . . . You know, I don't think your brain's getting enough ventilation.'

'How would you do it, Larry?' asked Frank.

'Don't encourage him, Frank! That's all we need, Larry comin' in one day with a machine gun down his trousers and an I've-been-pushed-too-far glint in his eye. Once he starts pullin' the trigger he's just the kind of person who's likely to think, "Oh yeah, I like this. This is me!"'

'How *would* you do it, Larry?' I asked, egging him on.

'Not you, too, Plato? Bleedin' hell. All right then, Larry. You might as well get it off yer chest. How would you do it? Bludgeon him to death in the library with the lead pipe?'

But Larry was suddenly coy.

'I'd rather not say at the moment.'

'Would you make it look like an accident?' Frank asked eagerly.

'Naturally.'

'Maybe he could fall out a window and break his neck?' he suggested helpfully. 'That'd be believable.'

'Course it would, Frank. Happens every day.'

'Maybe,' said Larry.

'Or maybe he could get crushed to death somehow?'

'Oh, good thinking, Frank. A pulpy, blood-dripping manager's sure not to arouse any suspicion. Commonplace, that kind of thing is. Well, I think you're both crazy! I think there might still be hope for you, Benton, but you're on the edge. You're teetering. You're on the cusp. I thought I was crazy, but you two are insane. You make my pet budgie look well adjusted, and he spends his time flying into brick walls. You know what you need, Larry? You need to get laid.'

'I've been laid,' said Larry defensively.

'It's not something you're supposed to do once, Larry – like havin' a cup of coffee on the Champs Élysées. You're supposed to do it regular like. You know, until you start to enjoy it.'

'The last time I enjoyed it was in 1978,' said Frank.

'Why was that, Frank?'

'I was thinking of something else.'

28

Strangely enough, not long after this conversation Sprigett was indeed found, if not exactly pulpy and dripping blood, at least dishevelled and unconscious, at the bottom of The Chamber of Horrors steps. Larry, who happened to be on duty there at the time was the first to find him and call for help. By the time an ambulance arrived, there was quite a little throng of guides and other staff milling about amongst the garrotted and disembowelled, not so much concerned as eager to catch a glimpse of the pompous little twerp dishevelled and unconscious at the bottom of a flight of stairs.

There was, however, no suspicion of foul play, or rather, there was no suspicion of foul play at first.

———

'What d'you mean, what have I done?' asked Larry later that day at lunch.

'There's no point being coy with me, Larry,' Vern told him. 'You've had that murderous glint in your eye all week. You've done for him, haven't you, you cold-blooded little killer, you? But don't worry, your secret is safe with me.'

'You're crazy. He tripped.'

'That's very convincing, Larry. Just stick with that story and everything should be just fine.'

'What? You think I pushed him? Yeah, right, Vern,' he said, a little too loudly, 'I hated his guts so I pushed the son of a bitch down the stairs.'

It wasn't until he'd filled his mouth with a great forkful of rubbery shepherd's pie and half masticated the hell out of it that he noticed the unnatural silence surrounding him and happened to glance up. What he saw when he did was the entire canteen, frozen in various states of goggle-eyed, slack-jawed amazement, staring, knives and forks in hand, at *him*.

'What did I say?'

———

The police were involved for a time, but only until Sprigett regained consciousness and could clear everything up. Of course, by that time Larry was sweating bullets, but we always knew he was innocent. Or at least we were reasonably certain he was innocent. Or rather, we were reasonably certain except for Frank.

'Well, Larry,' he said, unfortunately in front of half a dozen witnesses and one of the investigating officers, 'I'd just like to say I'm impressed! I never thought you had the ticker to actually go through with it.'

———

Sprigett made a full recovery, and was soon back at work, but not, as it turned out, for long. He was headhunted by Butlins.

We might have laughed about it (we did), and he might have been a pompous little twerp (he was), but the truth of the matter was that no one was about to headhunt me, or Vern, or Larry, and definitely not Frank, not even Butlins.

'You know, sometimes I lie awake at night wondering what the future might hold,' Vern said to me not long before I finally quit, 'and then I realise, it's this.' And then he asked me the question which actually made me do it. 'Tell me something, Ben,' he said, stirring what could have been his thousandth, or possibly ten thousandth cup of stewed, tepid, canteen tea. 'What are you doing here?'

'What d'you mean?'

'You started as a summer temp, right? What? Two years ago now?'

'Three,' I said.

'Well, look outside. It's snowing.'

———

The chances of someone ending up exactly where they are are mind-bogglingly astronomical, but of course no more mind-bogglingly astronomical than them ending up some place else. Wherever we are, at any given moment, the chances of us ever having got there remain head-spinningly uncomputational, but somehow we still do.

———

Vern won the Pools a couple of years after I'd left and bought a bar on some little dot of a Greek island. He didn't get many customers, but then again he didn't want many. He bought a yacht too, and learned to sail, and when he felt like it, would just shut up shop and go sailing for a few days, or a few weeks. Being Vern, he also took Larry and Frank with him.

It made a new man out of Larry.

'He even gets laid occasionally,' Vern wrote to me, 'and his temples have almost stopped throbbing.'

Frank, apparently, was missing his wife.

29

When I first met Cassie she had a cat, or to be more precise, up until very, very recently, she'd *had* a cat. Moments before this first meeting, this same cat – now ex-cat – suddenly decided to take a leap through an open fourth-floor living-room window to the street below. Apparently it used the sofa as a springboard, and sailed straight through without even touching the sides.

Strolling past at the time, I very nearly caught it, but didn't.

No sooner had I not caught it, and it not, despite what they say, landed on its feet, Cassie's head appeared behind it through this same open fourth-floor living-room window and screamed this:

'FLUFFYYYYYYYY!'

Sadly, not any more it wasn't.

———

Not knowing what else to say to someone whose cat had just plunged to its sticky death in front of me, I called out, 'Stay where you are. I'll bring it up.'

———

She took it hard, not surprisingly, and even more unsurprisingly once I'd heard the full story. 'I only turned my back for a second,' she said. 'And I thought the window was too high anyway.'

'You can hardly blame yourself,' I told her. 'It was just a freak accident.'

'But it wasn't an accident,' she said, still nursing Fluffy, whom I'd tactfully wrapped in my jacket before handing her over. 'I suspected she was planning something like this.'

'You suspected she was planning something like jumping out of a fourth-floor window?'

'Well, I didn't know how she'd do it, but I knew she'd try it again.'

'Try what again, exactly?'

'Killing herself, of course.'

Of course.

'What makes you think Fluffy killed herself?' I asked her, while at the same time trying to decide whether I had any kind of a chance with a girl this attractive, and if so, whether it was that great an idea anyway. After all, she'd just told me that her cat had committed suicide, and not even on its first attempt, which almost certainly qualified her as a deranged lunatic, and therefore under no circumstances whatsoever to be considered possible dating material, no matter how cute she was.

'It's happened before,' she said.

———

Cassie, it transpired, had a history of suicidal pets: a canary that managed to garrotte itself between the bars of its cage; a hamster which she found asphyxiated in her pants drawer; and a red setter that, upon reaching the stick she'd tossed into the shallows for it, just kept on going.

'And now Fluffy,' she sniffed.

'Well,' I said, thinking how well her short, rather boyish hair style showed off her lovely neck and pixie-ish features, and, needless to say, imagining her naked, 'I'm sure it's nothing personal. And anyway, you can't be certain it was suicide. It's not as if they left suicide notes or anything, is it. Is it?'

They hadn't, but as far as consoling words went, they weren't terribly effective, and I soon found myself in the unusually awkward position of sitting opposite a beautiful stranger whose sniffing had now turned to sobbing over her recently deceased cat which was still wrapped in my jacket while racking my brain for an appropriate way, if there was one, of excusing myself, with or without my jacket.

At last I managed to come up with this:

'Um.'

Then this:

'Well.'

And this:

'Right then.'

And finally, and most successfully, this:

'I guess I'll be off then.'

———

She pulled herself together enough to see me to the door, still cradling poor dead Fluffy wrapped in my jacket.

'You've been very kind,' she said.

'Don't mention it,' I told her.

'You must think I'm crazy.'

'Not at all,' I lied. 'I've heard far crazier things than someone thinking their cat committed suicide.'

'I meant the sobbing.'

'Of course. Well, you should've seen me when my goldfish died.'

'Oh, when did it die?'

'Not it. They. When I was six.'

'Oh.'

'They were murdered.'

'Oh! How horrible.'

'Squashed,' I said, then remembered Fluffy. 'Sorry.'

'That's all right.'

It didn't look as if she was going to mention it, so before I ended up possibly spending the rest of my life, or what would possibly just feel like the rest of my life, standing in her hallway with her and her dead cat, I did.

'Don't worry about the jacket,' I said, indicating the bundle in her arms.

'Oh, God. Your jacket. I didn't realise. It'll be ruined.'

'Doesn't matter.'

'Of course it matters. Is it leather?'

'Suede.'

'I'll have it dry-cleaned.'

'You don't have to,' I told her.

'Of course I do. I want to.'

'OK, then.'

'Can you come round and pick it up, or should I send it somewhere?'

'I can come round,' I said.

'It might take a few days. Suede's tricky.'

'So I believe.'

She looked down at the suede-clad bundle in her arms. Fluffy's head was just poking out the end. As far as a cat that had just apparently committed suicide by jumping from a fourth-floor window could she looked at peace. She might even have been asleep apart from the tiny pink tongue lolling out of one corner of her mouth, and a general flatness. 'I hope it'll be all right,' she said, her bottom lip beginning to tremble.

'Why don't I just take it with me now?' I suggested, then added hurriedly, as she started to sob again: 'Or you can just keep it. I've got plenty of jackets. I was actually thinking of getting rid of this one anyway. I almost never wear it. I don't even know why I was wearing it today. I've never even liked it. In fact, you should keep it – of course I don't mean keep it, because obviously you probably wouldn't feel all that comfortable wearing it after Fluffy's been – well, you know . . . What I mean is keep it for now, and then when you want to, just throw it away. Or not. Whatever.' On top of everything else, she was now actually crying into the jacket. 'I know,' I said. 'Why don't I just pop in one day next week? How's that?' Getting what might have been a nod, or possibly just part of a sob, I wrenched the door open and fled.

––––

The jacket, like Fluffy, was never quite the same again. In fact, I very nearly didn't even go back for it. I guess what finally overcame any reservations I had was the thought that she was probably really a very normal girl who had just been through a terribly traumatic experience and who would have gone to the trouble and expense of having it dry-cleaned and would be expecting me to pick it up and that there was always a slim possibility I'd end up having sex with her.

———

Fluffy wasn't replaced, or possibly she was, with me, but we did, eventually, despite our joint fears (hers of suicide, mine of murder), get another pet.

In fact we got two of them.

30

We called them Bing Bong and Sparkles, and they soon outgrew their original bowl and had to be moved into more palatial surroundings, commanding panoramic views of both the living room and kitchen, with filtered ones of the hall.

Popular wisdom has it that goldfish have a memory retention of only three seconds, and that they never get bored because by the time they've swum round their tank and got back to where they started from they've forgotten it. Not only is this a heinous slight to gold-fish, but, as anyone who has spent any quality time with their fish will testify, it couldn't be further from the truth.

Although not generally included in the top ten most intelligent animals (where the humble pig, incidentally, comes a surprising tenth place), with a bit of loving care and attention (and if they can avoid being squashed by fish-hating psychopaths), they will grow into extremely personable pets, complete with their own little quirks and idiosyncrasies. They like some music and don't respond to others (you have your rock fish and your classical fish, and quite probably your drum'n'bass and death metal fish as well). They can be moody and petu-lant, or as playful and frisky as a puppy, and they most definitely can recognise and identify people they know from people they don't, although they do seem to have trouble sometimes distinguishing between food and poo, which they often swallow by mistake, but nearly always spit out again.

———

I should have changed the channel as soon as it came on, of course, but I just didn't think. It was a programme about whales, and in particular why some whales, and sometimes whole pods of whales, despite being so intelligent, and it obviously not being that brilliant an idea, insist on beaching, and often re-beaching themselves. After watching it for an hour I still had no idea why they did it (except that it might have had something to do with shadowy military boffins who spent their time thinking up ever more outlandishly sneaky ways of being outlandishly sneaky), but after seeing all those beached whales drying out in the sun I felt in need of a good soak myself and went to run a bath.

———

From an early age it was impressed upon my brothers and me that under no circumstances were we to fall asleep in the bath. This, we were told, could only ever result in one thing: certain death. It was a surer way of drowning than waiting in an orderly manner for a place in a lifeboat on the *Titanic*. There were no two ways about it, apparently: fall asleep in the bath and you were a goner.

'You haven't fallen asleep in there, have you?' our mother would call out almost continuously from wherever she was in the house whenever any of us were having a bath.

'Not much chance of that with your mother around,' our father would joke.

One day, however, I decided to challenge the accepted wisdom.

'But if you were asleep, and your head slipped under the water, wouldn't the water wake you up?' I wanted to know.

'Just try it one of these days and see,' was my mother's chilling reply.

Of course I was never brave (or stupid) enough to put my theory to the test, and spent my childhood, whenever within the treacherous confines of a bathtub, upright and alert. Even as an adult, whenever I happened to doze off in the tub (the relaxing properties of a good bath bomb and a boring bath book eventually overcoming my mother's warning words) I would start awake again gulping for air.

———

I started awake gulping for air. 'I must stop doing that,' I told myself, before settling back again into the soothing warm water. Those whales must be bloody bonkers, I thought, and then I thought of *Moby Dick*, my bath book for the past three years (already a bit of a doorstopper, it had bloated to twice its original thickness owing to numerous accidental dunkings), and how, after three years of reading it, I still hadn't even got to the *Pequod* spotting the eponymous beast, much less getting to any kind of grips with it. The only other book that had ever taken me as long not to finish was *The Origin Of Species*, my one-time bedtime book. It took me nearly a year just to get past the pigeons, but at least I had a pretty good idea how it ended.

'All right, Ishmael,' I said, 'you windy bastard. I'll give you ten minutes to stop banging on about whale blubber steaks, or else that's it.'

I peeled it open at the appropriate place, and settled back. My eyes were just beginning to glaze over at even more delicious whale blubber recipes when I thought I heard something from outside.

In fact, I thought I heard a voice.

I listened.

Nothing.

Then I heard it again.

It was tiny, almost imperceptible, yet at the same time distraught, frantic even.

'*Help! Help!*' it was saying. '*He's drowning!*'

———

At first I thought I was dreaming. Then I thought I must have left the TV on. Then I realised I wasn't dreaming, and I hadn't left the TV on, but that I had left the top of the fish tank off when I'd last fed them, and I leapt out of the bath as if someone had just tossed an electric toaster in it (although in that case I would have merely shuddered and sizzled a bit, rather than actually leapt anywhere).

When I hit the kitchen linoleum, dripping wet as I was, my legs shot out from under me in a man-stepping-on-banana-peel pratfall of such sublime beauty it would have made Buster Keaton weep with joy. For a few moments I just lay there, in the middle of the kitchen floor, stark naked, stunned, confused, quite possibly concussed and generally racked with pain, and simply stared at the ceiling. I noticed I'd missed a bit of the cornicing in one corner when I'd recently repainted, then wondered what I was doing lying on my back in the middle of the kitchen floor staring at the ceiling thinking about cornicing, and then I remembered.

'*Help! Help! He's drowning!*'

I could still hear it, more urgent now than ever. Scrambling to my feet, I dashed to the fish tank. Sparkles, frantically bobbing up and down at the surface, I swear, did a back flip of joy when she saw me. On the other side of the glass, Bing Bong was lying in a little puddle on his side, his tail flapping weakly, his little gills gasping for air.

I scooped him up as gently as possible, and slipped him back into the water. He looked a little surprised, but not displeased to be there.

I put the lid back on the tank shakily, and collapsed on to the sofa. My heart was pounding, and I just lay there for a while watching them, Sparkles ricocheting about the tank like a shimmering golden bullet, and Bing Bong, now that he'd got his wind back, leisurely gliding back and forth as if nothing, and particularly nothing out of the ordinary, had just happened.

But I'd seen it.

I'd seen Skippy do it, and I'd seen Lassie do it, and now, Sparkles had done it too.

She'd saved the day.

31

At the time of strolling down Cassie's street and not catching her cat, I was living in a rather sinister-looking old house in Cricklewood in which a little feelgood movie called *Hellraiser* had been filmed some years before. Not being a big fan of horror films (unless they were made by Hammer, and preferably featuring sexy lesbian vampires), I hadn't seen it, but one night, at Cassie's insistence, we got it out on video.

It was a peculiarly unnerving experience watching the usual procession of hapless horror fodder being despatched in all manner of gruesomely inventive ways, their blood seeping under the floorboards to form some hideously nightmarish creature, and to realise that those very same floorboards under which the blood flowed and the creature gestated were my own. Cassie thought it was a riot, whereas I clearly had the wind up.

'I think I might have to move in with you,' I said to her when it was over, only half jokingly.

'OK,' she said.

And the next day we moved my stuff into her fourth-floor flat in Bayswater.

———

It wasn't quite as sudden as all that, as I had more or less been living with her for weeks, ever since the night we went and saw *Cats* (probably not the mostly tactful choice considering recent tragic events) and sang 'Islands in the Stream (That is What We Are)' at a pub karaoke afterwards.

But it was now official.

———

I'd never lived with anyone before, except Herman of course. And Bob. Herman and I were at college together, a time even more of a foreign country than the past. That is, not only do we do things differently there, but a lot of what we do (and say) makes absolutely no sense whatsoever. To wit, Herman was halfway through the collected works of Shakespeare – not reading them, you understand, but eating them (something to do with ingesting genius). He also had two extra toes and grand literary ambitions (writing as well as eating), and was fond of saying things like, 'Aeschylus! Shakespeare! Ibsen! Beckett! Men of vision! Of integrity! Of deep and penetrating thought! Men who would suffer any pains, any torment, who would endure – *nay*, relish! – deprivation, discomfort and hardship. And for what? For the sake of their art, for the sake of their vocation, for the sake of their sacred duty to mankind! . . . I am the inheritor of that long and glorious tradition. I am the direct descendant of that noble lineage. I, Herman Skog, am a serious playwright!' whenever the subject of rent, housework, lectures or personal hygiene came up. Not being overly keen on paying, doing or attending the first three myself (although I did wash regularly), we subsequently lived in a cosy and perpetual state of impending eviction, encroaching squalor and last-minute, desperate cramming.

And then, one day (somewhere around Mark Antony's speech to the plebs, I recall), the door bell rang.

I answered it to find a stranger, and a strange stranger at that, about my own age, holding a battered suitcase in one hand and an equally battered violin case in the other. Rather surprisingly, he stepped straight inside, right past me, before putting down the suitcase, swapping the violin case to his other hand, and then thrusting out his free hand in greeting.

'Bob!' he said.

'Sorry?'

At the sound of my voice he swung around to face me, as he had until then been holding his hand out into empty space.

'I'm Bob.'

I shook his hand tentatively.

'Hi, Bob. I'm Benton.'

'Hi, Benton,' he said.

'And that's Herman,' I said, nodding towards the sofa.

'Who is?' asked Bob.

'Over here on the sofa,' said Herman.

Bob waved in his general direction as if he were waving to a ship at sea.

'Hi, Herman!' he called cheerily.

'Hi, Bob,' Herman called back, before mouthing at me, 'Who the hell is this?'

I shrugged back at him.

'So . . . Bob?' I said.

'Yes, Benton?'

'Can we . . . do anything in particular for you today?'

'What did you have in mind?' he asked.

'Well, I don't know, really,' I faltered. 'Herman?'

'Maybe a glass of water to help wash down his pills?' Herman suggested helpfully.

'No, I think I'm fine actually. I don't want you to think you have to put yourselves out. I'm very easy to get along with. I'm sure I'll be very happy here.'

'Happy?' I said.

'Here?' said Herman.

He gazed about the room. 'From what I can see, it looks quite delightful.' He took a step and walked into a bookcase. 'By the way, should I just give the rent to you? A month in advance, wasn't it?'

The occasional odd, to very odd, character turning up at our door wasn't in itself unheard of, of course. A guy dressed in bin liners and WWI flying goggles once rang the bell to ask if he could pitch his wigwam on our doorstep. When I told him there wasn't really enough room, he said it was only a small wigwam. We even had a regular loony. Every couple of weeks there would be a knock on the door, we'd answer it, and out he'd jump from behind a bush in his underpants, shouting, 'Shazam!'

Having them offer to pay us money, however, was a new and interesting development. The fact that it had to be a misunderstanding rather than a wadded-up nutcase dawned on us both at about the same time, but whereas I was just about to put our would-be share-mate right with a quick shove out the door, Herman, being Herman, had other ideas.

'Actually, Bob,' he said, 'two months would be better.'

Unfortunately there were only two bedrooms, one of which was mine when I went to the toilet, but was Bob's by the time I came out again.

'So where am I supposed to sleep?'

'The sofa is probably the least uncomfortable piece of furniture, so I'd sleep there,' suggested Herman.

'Then why don't you?' I suggested back.

'Because Bob's not in my room.'

'And when was this decided? When I was in the toilet. I hardly call that a democratic decision.'

'You decided to go to the toilet,' said Herman.

I started violently awake exactly like someone being woken from a deep sleep in the middle of the night by a complete stranger suddenly launching into a fast and furious rendition of Vivaldi's *Four Seasons* approximately two and a half feet from their left ear, except I don't suppose Bob could be called a complete stranger as he'd just handed over two months' rent up front for the privilege of sleeping in what until very recently had been my bed.

The first thing I did was fall off the sofa.

Before I had time to do anything else except bang my head on the floor, the living-room light snapped on.

'What the *hell* is going on?' Herman demanded, his crusty, unwashed hair sticking out at assorted and interesting angles.

Standing approximately two and a half feet from my left ear was our new lodger, bollock naked, playing his violin like summer itself depended on it. Sitting on the floor two and a half feet away from him, as I was, and what with him being bollock naked, as he was, and roused (he must have *really* liked Vivaldi), I scrambled speedily to my feet and joined Herman, who was by this time regarding the whole spectacle with rather wry astonishment.

'He plays the violin in his sleep,' he said ruefully. 'The answer to all our financial woes plays the violin in his sleep.'

'He nearly gave me a fucking heart attack!' I said.

'Bob?' Herman said gently. '*BOB?*'

'Isn't it dangerous to wake someone when they're sleepwalking?' I asked.

'He's standing still.'

'What if he turns violent? I've heard that can happen.'

'Well, there are two of us if he does.'

'Doesn't a suddenly woken sleepwalker have the strength of ten men?' I asked.

'Where do you get this stuff?'

'I pick it up here and there,' I told him.

There was a sudden hammering on the wall, and an irate just-been-woken-up-in-the-middle-of-the-night-by-those-fucking-students-next-door voice. 'Hey, Vivaldi!' it said. 'Shut the fuck up!'

'Vivaldi. Of course,' said Herman. '*The Four Seasons.*'

'I know,' I said.

'Actually, he's quite good.'

A string suddenly broke, and he stopped playing instantly. He replaced the violin in its case, picked it up and returned to his room, closing the door behind him.

The next morning, at breakfast, Bob informed us he couldn't remember the last time he'd slept so well.

'Really?' I asked. 'You weren't a bit – restless?'

'Not at all. Slept like a baby. I can almost understand what Herman meant when he told me why you were giving up your bed.'

'Um,' I said. 'And why was that, again – exactly?' I asked, sticking out a leg to prevent Herman, who had begun to edge towards the door, from leaving.

'You thought it was too comfortable,' said Bob.

'Sorry?'

'Remember?' said Herman. 'How you said all those wonderful nights' sleep were beginning to interfere with your social life? How you'd be at a great party having a fantastic time and you'd suddenly remember how comfortable your bed was and rush home to go to sleep?'

Before I could make a suitably pithy reply, or maybe just pithily punch him in the testicles, Bob piped up. 'I went to a party last week,' he announced chirpily. 'At least I think it was a party.'

'So, Bob?' said Herman, after a pause.

'Yes, Herman?'

'I see you're wearing glasses this morning.'

'Ah, that's how I found the kitchen,' he said. 'You probably didn't notice yesterday, but I have slightly less than perfect vision.'

'No?' we both said.

'Well, I'm very intuitive. I sense my surroundings. In fact I probably don't really need them,' he said, taking them off and putting them in his bowl of Shreddies. 'As you can see.' He felt around for his glasses again, before

I quietly removed them from his bowl of cereal and placed them by his hand. He found them again and put them on. A small trickle of milk dribbled down the side of his nose.

'So, you're a musician?' I asked.

'That's right.'

'I suppose you have to practise a lot, then?' asked Herman.

'I know what you're thinking,' said Bob, earnestly. 'You're thinking: Musician – Practice – The End of Peace and Tranquillity. Well, let me put your minds at ease. You've got nothing to fear.' He paused, rather dramatically, before adding, as if about to impart a great secret. 'I *don't*.'

'You don't what?' I asked.

'Practise.'

'You don't practise?'

'Never,' he said.

'Never?'

'Never,' said Bob, his face assuming a near beatific puzzlement. 'And yet,' he paused, 'I'm sure I'm getting better.'

———

I eventually got my room back after Bob eloped with a girl he met in a music store while trying to buy chocolate croissants.

'Eight chocolate croissants, my good man,' he'd said.

'Excuse me?' said his wife-to-be.

'Oh!' said Bob. 'You're a woman.'

'Not bad for a second guess. And we don't sell croissants, chocolate or otherwise. We're a music store.'

'Ah! Then you'd probably sell violin strings.'

32

Living with Cassie was nice, although apart from Herman and Bob I didn't really have anything much to compare it with. Georgia and I, despite all our years together, had never actually lived together, and even when I'd slept over it usually necessitated a quick dawn getaway before her parents had time to wake up and catch us in flagrante and thus realise that I was, and probably had been for some time past, in the habit of casually despoiling their very own daughter beneath their very own roof. At first I used to clamber up the side of the house to her bedroom window, but as it soon became apparent clambering wasn't really one of my strong points (or indeed Georgia's as it turned out), she had a spare back-door key cut and would lower it down to me on a piece of string when I came round after lights out. I would hide in a convenient bush, Huck Finn like, and hoot like an owl, or rather, hoot like someone who thought they knew how to hoot like an owl, and down it would come. I'd silently let myself in, lock the door behind me, and tippy-toe upstairs to commence my illicit despoiling, thus proving myself a much better creeper than clamberer, which may or may not be significant.

But living with Cassie, as I say, was nice. It was so nice that, while I was witness to a seemingly endless procession of teachers coming and going – from this or that exotic overseas teaching position to some even more exotic overseas teaching position – brimming with photos and anecdotes and sun tans and terrible drawstring trousers, I was happy to stay put, exactly where I was, next to Cassie.

———

My parents loved her from the start, naturally. They also thought she was just what I needed, which is just the kind of thing parents usually think when their offspring are a bit rubbish and they manage to land someone decidedly unrubbish to spend their lives with. If they ever found out I'd cheated on her, they would probably disown me, or, as Ray put it: 'You better hope Mum never finds out because if she does she'll kick your arse from here to next week.'

———

Lying, an integral part of cheating, is like falling off a log, only easier. But each time you fall off, you've got to land somewhere, and sometimes it's on your feet, and sometimes it's on your backside, and sometimes it's in a great big pile of steaming dog shit, and you come up smelling, or convinced you're smelling, so bad you're amazed you're still accepted in polite society. And yet you are – it's as if no one even notices. The trick, then, is to pretend you don't notice it either.

Of course, I was lying on two fronts, which can be tricky, and sometimes I wasn't altogether sure whether

I was lying or not, which can be tricky *and* confusing, plus I had more than a sneaking suspicion, right from the start, that I was actually telling myself the biggest porky pies of all, which is tricky, confusing, *and* worrying, because if you can't trust yourself, who can you trust?

———

How people keep up double lives for years I have no idea. Apart from everything else, it must be exhausting. The sudden realisation that I myself was leading one, could, and often did, bring me up short in the middle of the most mundane activities – making a cup of tea or cleaning my teeth – and I would just stand there, mind boggling at the mere thought, the unbelievability of it, while the same burning question throbbed like a crazily insistent second pulse over and over in my head: '*What the hell am I doing, what the hell am I doing?*'

33

'What's she like?'

'Who?' I asked.

'Your girlfriend.'

It was the first time Cherry had ever asked anything about her, straight out like this. She'd never met her, obviously, or even seen a photo of her (I thought it only good etiquette to take down the handful of photos of the two of us scattered about the flat the time I invited her round to deflower). She never asked anything about her, and I never volunteered anything. Cassie was just something that existed between us, a hurdle, but at that time a by no means insurmountable one, which we just had to get over the best way we could to gain the rich, green pastures beyond. For that was where we definitely saw ourselves headed – those rich, green pastures of the future, a future where we would be together, a proper couple, able to do proper couple-type things. There would be no more need for sneaking around. No need to be constantly covering my tracks. No need for those heart-stopping moments when, strolling with Cherry somewhere I shouldn't have been, or some time I shouldn't have been, I saw, or thought I saw, someone Cassie and I knew. Cherry was patient, understanding, and, most of all, undemanding. She would never call me at home; she didn't even want my phone number. We would say goodbye on Friday, and see each other again

144

on Monday. It was a working week, office hours (with occasional overtime) affair.

But of course it couldn't stay that tidy forever.

'She's nice,' I said.

'What does she do?'

'That's a good question.'

'Why? You don't know?'

'Well, not exactly,' I admitted, a little embarrassed. 'I kind of know, but I'm a little vague about the details. She's some kind of consultant.'

It was true. In fact, I was more than a little vague about the details, I really had no idea what she did, how she spent her days. Of course I already knew I didn't know this, but suddenly being asked, unexpectedly, out of the blue like that, threw me. Why didn't I know this? How could I not know what she did? She must have talked about her work, must have been talking about it for years, yet here I was, when asked, unable to furnish anything more enlightening than 'Some kind of consultant.' But what did people actually consult her about? I made a mental note to find out.

'What else?'

'What else do you want to know?'

'What does she look like?' she asked, then quickly changed her mind. 'No – I don't want to know. What kind of things does she like?'

'What does she like?' I had to think for a moment. 'Meerkats,' I said.

'Whatcats?'

'Meerkats. They're like a cute rat. Or gopher. But not really. They're from Africa, I think. Anyway, she's crazy about them.'

'What else?'

'I don't know. Woody Allen movies – the early ones, of course. *Love & Death*. *Sleeper*. *Annie Hall*. Her all-time favourite scene in the world ever has to be the giant banana peel in *Sleeper* where Woody and the guy chasing him keep slipping over on it. Then he knocks him out with a giant strawberry.'

'What else?'

'What else? Peanut butter and lettuce sandwiches. And hot English mustard. And musicals – the cornier the better. *Seven Brides for Seven Brothers*. *Brigadoon*. And disco – real disco. And Miss Marple mysteries. And greasy spoon breakfast blowouts. And *Malory Towers*. And dappled sunlight. And the Sunday papers in bed. And –'

I stopped suddenly.

'Go on,' said Cherry.

But I didn't want to. I had inadvertently summoned her up by this simple recitation of silly, seemingly insignificant likes, which could have, I realised, continued to tumble out of me all day if left unchecked, until she was there, with us, or at least with me, in a way she hadn't been before. I felt a sudden hollow feeling in the pit of my stomach. How, I wondered, could I live without all those things? The sound of her voice on the answering machine when she called and I wasn't in ('Hello, hello? Are you there? You're not there? Oh, you're not there . . .'). Or the way she creaked the bedroom door back and forth with her foot to attract my attention weekends when she finally surfaced and needed tea.

These things were her, and now, already, before I'd even lost them, I was missing them, and knew I would miss a hundred, a thousand, a hundred thousand other equally stupid things about her as well.

But that's not to say she didn't drive me crazy sometimes.

She did.

34

'No smile for me,' she said.

Cassie's younger brother, Allsop, was getting married, and we were to catch the train up for the weekend. The wedding was in Hambledon, a place I'd been familiar with ever since I was a kid, not just because I'd broken my arm falling through my grandparents' roof picking plums there, but because it was such a scenic little spot it often appeared on TV, as well as being home to the pond that Truly Scrumptious drove into and had to be carried, protestingly, out of by Dick Van Dyke in *Chitty Chitty Bang Bang*.

'I smiled,' I said, although in considerable pain, having put my back out in an overly athletic session with Cherry the day before.

I'd arrived at the station at the designated time and spent the past fifteen minutes watching a clock ticking off the seconds to the next train, feeling increasingly tetchy because I hadn't had any lunch. Of course I could easily have bought something, and would have done except I didn't want to hump my bag over to the shops, but leave it with Cassie, which I couldn't do because she was late.

'We've got ten minutes to the next train,' I said, with just a hint of reproof.

'Plenty of time,' she said.

'Well, I don't know about plenty of time, but hopefully

it's enough to get something to eat. I'm starving,' I told her. 'Do you want anything?'

'I'll come with you.'

'Just tell me what you want and I'll get it. You mind the bags.'

'Nothing,' she said.

'Really? You don't want anything?'

'I packed us a picnic.'

'You did? Well, why didn't you say so?'

'It's not for now. It's for the trip. So if you're hungry now . . .'

'The train leaves in ten minutes. I'm sure I can survive for another ten minutes,' I said, a little exasperated. 'Of course I'd prefer a picnic.'

But, for whatever reasons – a bad day at the office, her baby brother getting married, the time of the month even – it was too late. Her face had dropped. Her eyes began to well with tears.

'What? What have I done? There's no reason to cry. Nothing's happened!' I burbled. 'God, I hate it when you do this. This is ridiculous! Why are you crying?'

'I'm not crying,' she said. 'Why are you shouting at me?'

'Who's shouting? This isn't shouting. This is talking. Shouting's much louder. People shout when they're angry. I'm not angry. Why would I be angry?'

'I don't know why you're angry.'

'I'm not angry. Who said I was angry?'

'You did. Just then.'

'What?'

'Listen to yourself. You're angry. And you're shouting.'

'I'm starting to get angry now, but I wasn't angry before. And I'm still not shouting.'

'Come on. We're going to miss our train.'

But it wasn't over yet.

'I wasn't angry,' I said, once we were settled in our seats.

'Fine. You weren't angry.'

'And I never shouted.'

'Fine.'

'I really didn't do anything wrong, you know. I was just hungry and wanted to get something to eat. You should've just said you had a picnic straightaway when I said I wanted to get something to eat.'

'Can we drop it?'

'I just don't see that there was any reason for you to start crying.'

'Can you stop, please?'

'I'm sorry, but it's not rational.'

'Right!' she said.

'What are you doing?'

She had started to gather up her stuff.

'I'm getting off.'

'You can't get off. The train's about to leave.'

She tried to get past me. It must have been about a minute before we were due to depart.

'Can you move, please?'

I tried to reason with her.

'You're crazy!' I told her. 'You're being ridiculous.'

'Will you *move*, please!'

'Well, there's no bloody point you getting off, is there? It's your wacko brother who's getting married,' I said, not shouted, dragging my bag down from the luggage rack. 'I'll get off.'

'Fine.'

'Fine. Good. Great.'
And I got off.

I watched the train pull out and away from the plat-form, with Cassie on board sitting next to an empty seat where moments before I'd been sitting, and asked myself, 'How has this happened?' Then I thought about the picnic, and wondered what might have been in it, and felt the first stab of remorse, not because I was hungry, although I was, or because I thought I had been in the wrong, which I guess I also was, but because I knew how much Cassie loved a picnic, and how excited she would have been buying everything, putting it together for the train journey. There would be sandwiches, a scotch egg maybe, crisps, a Twix for her and probably a Turkish Delight for me, and pop of course. I wondered whether she would still eat it, and if she did, whether it would make her miserable, and what she would do with mine. She might eat the Turkish Delight, I guessed, but she would most probably have got salami sand-wiches for me, or possibly coronation chicken, and she wasn't so keen on salami, and she couldn't stand coro-nation chicken, so she would probably just throw them away. She'd definitely eat the crisps though, I thought. And then I picked up my bag and went to see if I could buy another ticket.

35

Not long after Cassie and I started going out, this same brother went away to college only to then completely and utterly disappear off the face of the planet. It was his first real time away from home and his parents, understandably, were more than a little anxious. When no trace of him could be found, they contacted the police. The police couldn't find him, either. His parents, by this time, were no longer anxious, they were frantic. Cassie herself was convinced he'd been murdered and dismembered, and his limbs and torso packed inside a suitcase abandoned at the left-luggage at Charing Cross. I remember it was Charing Cross because I remember being surprised when she told me, not so much by the gruesomeness of the hypothesis – although it was certainly that – as by its preciseness.

As it turned out, the family received a phone call three weeks later from none other than the missing person himself, asking to be picked up. They found him sitting on the kerb at the designated spot, dressed in nothing but a pair of white underpants (new!), with a small brown suitcase beside him.

He had absolutely no explanation as to where he'd been.

That night, after everyone had been contacted who needed to be contacted, and the family (including Cassie) were all sleeping soundly under the same roof again, an ear-splitting wailing suddenly shattered the peace. For five minutes the family proceeded to race around the house in various stages of panic and undress, searching for the source of the ungodly commotion, which showed no signs of abating.

Only Allsop slept soundly on.

At last, however, the offending noise was tracked down. It was coming from Allsop's room. It was, in fact, coming from his small brown suitcase. Naturally, it was locked.

'I can't hear myself think!' cried Cassie's and Allsop's father, holding his hands over his ears.

'*Sshh*!' their mother hissed at him. 'You'll wake Allsop.'

'I'll get the bolt cutters,' said Cassie.

When she returned and they'd cut the locks off the suitcase, they found a beautifully detailed alarm clock in the shape of a mosque inside. Instead of the more usual, gently annoying *beepbeepbeep* of your average or common or garden variety alarm clock, however, it was emitting an extraordinarily authentic-sounding, and continuous, wailing: the traditional Muslim summons to prayer.

Apart from that, though, the suitcase was totally, utterly, and indeed, completely, empty.

———

Nothing particularly out of the ordinary occurred at the wedding, except for the fact that both bride and groom wore *Star Trek* uniforms. But that night, their wedding night, an unforgivable yet inspired act of bastardry was perpetrated upon them. After the festivities were over, and everyone had retired to their respective beds, or otherwise, the newlyweds were suddenly jolted awake by the sound of an alarm clock going off somewhere in their room. After their initial surprise, they groggily tried to focus on where the annoying sound was coming from, finally tracking it down inside the little kettle provided for their tea- and coffee-making convenience.

It was 1 a.m.

The next rude awakening came exactly quarter of an hour later, perfectly timed so that they'd had just long enough to lapse back into a deep sleep. The source of the muffled clanging was once again groggily searched for and found, but with rather more difficulty this time as it was ingeniously concealed inside the Gideon Bible in one of the bedside drawers. The fiend, or fiends responsible had actually cut out a section and fitted the small alarm clock inside it.

This was repeated twice more before the by now frantic and sleep-deprived couple decided to just search the whole room once and for all in one big sweep, which they did.

They found a total of fifteen assorted alarm clocks, all set at fifteen-minute intervals, which was unfortunate as there were sixteen.

At five o'clock, on the dot, after a ragged night of sheer hell, they were woken one last time, but not by the usual, gently annoying *beepbeepbeep* of your average or common or garden variety alarm clock, but by an extraordinarily authentic-sounding, and continuous, wailing: the traditional Muslim summons to prayer.

Cursing friends and family alike, and anyone else who could have been responsible, in sturdy Anglo-Saxon as well as Klingon, Cassie's brother finally found it in his own suitcase, packed and ready for the honeymoon, while his hysterical new bride sobbed quietly into her pillow.

36

Having temporarily lost her brother not long after we started going out, Cassie soon lost her father, too, this time rather more permanently, which was difficult for everyone, especially him.

It was all very sudden.

His car was hit by a train, although that's not what killed him.

———

After her brother's mysterious disappearance and even more mysterious re-appearance, Cassie's parents and he were taking a therapeutic drive in the country when their car stalled on a deserted railway crossing. After attempting to re-start it a number of times, to no avail, Cassie's mother and brother jumped out to push while their father steered. They had nearly, but not quite managed to get it clear of the tracks when a train suddenly appeared. It braked, naturally, but kept on coming. Cassie's mother and brother leaped clear at the last moment, but her father, who was a careful man (which made the fact of his being killed by stalling, of all places, on a railway crossing rather ironic) was not only still wearing his seatbelt, but had his door locked as well, as had been his custom at all times for fear of car jackers since reading about a spate of cases in Miami.

The train only just clipped the tail of the car, but still managed to flip it and send it into such a terrifying spin that a witness later reported that it actually made him dizzy.

When, at last, after what seemed a very long time, the car finally stopped spinning, the train had ground to a halt, Cassie's mother and brother had had time to pick themselves up off the ground where they'd flung themselves, and the above-mentioned witness had had to sit down due to his similarly above-mentioned dizziness.

For a long moment nothing happened. No one moved. Not Cassie's mother and brother. Not the dizzy witness. Not the train driver who had leapt down from the driver's car. Not even the long row of passengers' faces pressed up against the carriage windows in open-mouthed incredulity.

Then there was the sound of a door lock being flipped, and the driver's door of the upside-down car creaked open complainingly. Cassie's father half clambered, half tumbled out, and stood there a little unsteadily on his feet.

It was a miracle!

He was alive!

In fact, there wasn't a scratch on him.

'Well, fuck me,' he said, using the F-word in front of his family for the first and only time in his life. Then he clutched his chest and keeled over, dead on the spot.

———

There are a couple of things with a new boyfriend or girlfriend that could justifiably be called tough breaks.

The all-time doozy would have to be landing one who, before you're even comfortable farting in front of them, is diagnosed with a terminal disease or suffers a crippling accident. A death in the family, although not in the same league, is also a drag. Obviously, these things can't really be helped, although strictly speaking collisions with trains can, and generally should be.

———

I think in many ways your partner dying, suddenly and unexpectedly (and preferably as painlessly as possible, naturally), is probably easier to deal with than if they drag on for a while first. Likewise with comas, paralysis, wasting diseases, and insanity (amongst others). I can only imagine what Georgia's and my life together would have been like if she hadn't frozen to death after breaking her neck, and she'd been farting in front of me for years.

———

Cassie didn't have a terminal disease, and wasn't in any way physically incapacitated, but I still sometimes imagined, or daydreamed, while she was out, and especially late returning home, that she had met with some devastating accident (always fatal, no malingering). Of course this did have some antecedence in the whole dead-fiancée incident, but I don't think it was just that, as, coincidently or not, this daydreaming tendency showed a pronounced blossoming once I became involved with Cherry. Even I have to admit there might have been a bit of wish fulfilment there, if not any real malice. That is, I in no way whatsoever wished Cassie dead, but at the same time I couldn't, on occasion, help entertaining quite elaborate fantasies constructed around just such an eventuality. Of course within these fantasies I was always suitably devastated, although my devastation was usually of the bravely internalised variety rather than the flashy going-to-pieces type, and always allowed for a more than respectable time to elapse before inevitably embarking on a brave new life with Cherry. This scenario was irresistible as far as guilt-free break-ups went, permitting me to segue from the old, familiar relationship to the new, sexually charged one without so much as an it's-not-you-it's-me conversation. In my defence, however, I would usually no sooner find myself in Cherry's tinglingly exciting embrace than my until then Rip Van Winkle-like conscience would suddenly lumber awake to pop, pin-like, the whole Mills & Boon soufflé.

That, or else the sound of Cassie's key in the lock.

37

Just as movie stars look taller than they are, and people look fatter on TV, busting down doors looks a lot easier than it is. Only after first nearly dislocating a shoulder, then almost breaking half the bones in my foot, did I remember what a locksmith once showed me years before when he was fitting a deadlock to my door after I had just been burgled. With a spring lock, all anyone has to do is slip a credit card, or if they can't be trusted with a credit card, a laminated library card will do, against the lock, between the door and the doorframe, and press. If you know what you're doing, or if you're incredibly lucky, it just might pop open, and your seriously screwed-up relationship, depending on whether you can explain how the burglars got in, account for why nothing was stolen, retrace the trajectory of your condom as it shot across the room, find your other girlfriend's missing underwear, and live with yourself after what you've done, might, just might be rescued from the gaping jaws of otherwise certain doom.

———

'My God!' I said, once I'd got the bag off her head, un-Sellotaped her, weathered the terrifying fit of trembling and body-racking sobs that suddenly gripped her, and generally held and comforted her while she spluttered her way through her version of recent events as experienced from the inside of a large plastic bin bag. 'It's unbelievable!' And then, before she had time to recall it herself, I asked wonderingly, 'But how did they get in?'

'They must have forced the lock,' she said.

'They couldn't have forced the deadlock,' I pointed out, dangerously.

'Maybe you didn't lock it properly this morning when you left.'

'It's possible, I guess,' I mused thoughtfully, and then, with all the feigned horror of full realisation, added, 'God, then this is my fault! God, I'm so sorry, baby.'

'Don't be silly, you just forgot to lock the door. You didn't attack me.'

'I know, but still . . . '

'Of course it wasn't your fault,' she reassured me, and then, beginning to cry softly, 'God, I was so scared, Ben.'

'I know you were, baby,' I said, holding her tight and scanning the area behind her for underwear and condoms. I'd found the keys where I'd dropped them, but the other two items were still causing me more than a little anxiety. I hadn't dared risk even the most cursory search before 'rescuing' her in case she heard me (admittedly this was unlikely over her nerve-shredding screams for help, but she had to stop to draw breath some time), and so just had to hope I found them before she did.

_____

I saw the condom first. It had certainly got some elevation, as it was hanging from the end of a curtain rail.

161

Retrieving it for the moment was out of the question, however, so I just held her tighter, my mind racing. If I let her go, I thought, she might lie back on the bed, from which position the dangling prophylactic would be in clear view. Then again, sitting up holding her like this, I was leaving the whole other side of the bedroom dangerously exposed to her scrutiny, should she have recovered sufficiently to scrutinise.

And a pair of tiny pink pants (with bows, I seemed to remember), once scrutinised, would be far less easily explained away than an unforced door.

I had to think hard, and I had to think fast.

'What about a nice cuppa tea?' I said.

———

Of course she wanted to call the police, and of course I convinced her that there was no point. After all, nothing had been stolen, no one was actually hurt, and she hadn't seen so much as an intruder's pinky (although considerably more than that had been on show). Instead I sat her down with a nice, strong cup of tea and a biscuit, nipped back into the bedroom and pocketed the errant condom (resisting the temptation to flush it down the toilet: they almost never flush first go), and had a quick – but not quick enough – rummage about on the floor and under the bed for Cherry's missing pants.

'What are you doing?' she asked, suddenly appearing in the doorway.

I heard her a nano-second before she did, which although not giving me enough time to leap back to my feet and assume a slightly more natural position than that of on my hands and knees rummaging under a bed, did at least give me enough time to grab my leg.

'Argh!' I groaned, feigning agony. 'Cramp!'

———

The missing pants eventually showed up about a week later, although, as it turned out, they were never really missing. After turning not only the bedroom but the entire flat upside-down looking for them, I happened to sneeze in class one day, and feeling about in my pockets for a handkerchief produced, to my students' great amusement and Cherry's and my even greater amazement, the pair of pants in question.

I had obviously slipped them into my pocket after slipping them off her (I remembered then that I'd undressed her first) either because I suspected they would be just the sort of thing most likely, and dangerously, to go missing in the general melee of clothes shedding, or else I was sicker than I thought and wanted them as a keepsake.

38

My mother's mother, forever Nan to my brothers and me, and nothing but a kind, gentle, radiant presence all our young lives, was, in an earlier incarnation, according to her daughter, our mother, a half-to-three-quarters crazed tyrant and firebrand. With her crop of dark, unruly hair and almost black, messianic eyes, this description of her, although seemingly rather fanciful, became considerably more feasible when you looked at the few surviving photos of her from that time. It must be said she did have something of a female, more handsome Charles Manson about her, which isn't necessarily a bad thing when you consider how close he came to being one of the Monkees.

One night, after having uncharacteristically defied my future Nan-to-be in the matter of attending a local knees-up, or Bacchanalian debauch, my meek, mild, and at twenty-five, unnaturally obedient mother returned home, just shy of turning into a pumpkin, to find herself not only locked out, but the entire contents of her room, bed included, sitting in the front garden.

My brother Truman was born at home, my mother's mother died there, in the same bed, nine years later. My mother, obviously present at the first event, was also there for the second.

'What is it, Mum? What's the matter?' she had asked, as Nan pushed back the bedclothes and tried to sit up. 'Are you too hot?' But she wasn't too hot, nor was there anything the matter, apart from the fact she was very shortly about to draw her last breath. The long hard years had dropped away from her face, and in her eyes, those dark, messianic eyes of old, which were now so obviously gazing upon a different world than that which appeared to surround them, was, my mother has said, a look of the most complete, resounding, and absolute peace.

And then, with the tiniest sigh, her life left her body.

'When it's my time to go,' my mother has maintained ever since, 'I won't be afraid, because I know there's something wonderful waiting there.'

————

When my mother was caught short with Truman, and found herself in bed, in labour and incapable of getting to the hospital, she had to bellow for a full ten minutes before she attracted anyone's attention, and even then it was only four-year-old Raymond who through cool idle curiosity just happened to pop his head in to see what all the fuss was about. What he found was his frantic, sweating, screaming, hyperventilating mother, and it was only through the direst threats of annihilation that she prevented him from immediately taking to his heels as if fleeing from a wild, slavering beast casually come upon in a most unexpected place. Once she had frozen the very marrow of his bones with these most unmotherly threats, she told him, in gentler tones now, as his initial terror and understandable urge to flee turned to injured bewilderment, and began to manifest itself in quivering lips and brimming eyes, to get help. At this he was off like a shot, and soon returned, to his mother's everlasting gratitude, with the cavalry, or in this case, our next-door neighbours.

Living on one side of us were the Binghams, and on the other, Mr and Mrs Papadopoulos. Mr Bingham arrived first, bursting through the bedroom door like, as my mother remembers it, some mild-mannered suburban superhero. My mother loved him at that moment. Never has she, before or since, been so over-joyed to see another human being, my soon-to-be-delivered brother included. But the sight that greeted him, no less than it had my infant eldest brother, turned him to jelly, and if it hadn't been for Mrs Tom (as we called Mrs Papadopoulos, after her greengrocer husband, Tom) arriving hard on his heels, and literally blocking the doorway behind him, he may well have taken to them.

'Albert, Albert!' my mother implored Mr Bingham, desperately, clutching his hand in an iron grip. 'You'll have to deliver the baby.'

The blood drained from his face.

'I – I – I –' he stammered, his previous mild-manneredness dissolved to bug-eyed terror, 'I'll call the doctor!' And with that he wrenched his hand free (not an easy thing; he had the embarrassing tell-tale signs of my mother's grip for days) and was gone. Unfortunately in his near blind panic to get away he fell down the stairs and broke his leg, but still managed to drag himself to the phone and call the doctor.

'Don't leave me, Mrs Tom,' pleaded my mother, gripping her hand in hers. 'Don't leave me!'

Mrs Tom sat on the edge of the bed and stroked my mother's fevered brow.

'Poor Mrs Kirby,' she said soothingly. 'Poor Mrs Kirby.'

Then she went to get up, but my mother's grip tightened like a vice. 'No worry, Mrs Kirby. I stay. I stay.'

My mother relaxed her grip and Mrs Tom stood up and began to rummage about the room.

'Are you looking for something in particular?' asked my bewildered mother, still half fearful Mrs Tom was about to do a runner, but going about it in a rather more craftily convoluted way than the hapless Albert, grimacing in agony downstairs.

'A scissor,' said Mrs Tom simply. 'Ah! I find one.'

She returned to the bed with the scissors, pulled open my mother's top, and deftly snipped the two over-the-shoulder bra straps, leaving the two bra cups still sitting perfectly in place. Whatever the reasoning behind such an unusually enigmatic procedure my mother never got to know, because our father-to-be suddenly appeared in the room, having seemingly leapt from the bottom landing in a single bound, and what with one thing and another, she never thought to ask afterwards.

39

Mrs Tom came over from Greece to marry Nick, the owner of our local fish-and-chip shop, but fell in love with Tom, the owner of our local greengrocer's, and married him instead. Nick never really got over this, and remained a bachelor to his dying day, doing little except endlessly battering and frying fish (and more than occasionally re-frying it, or even re-re-frying it), from which one might safely conclude Mrs Tom, before she became Mrs Tom, made a pretty wise choice marrying who she did and not marrying who she didn't.

Although this all happened long before I was born, I seemed always to have known these most intimate details about them, and it definitely cast the three of them in a considerably more romantic light than was probably usual for a small boy to view his local fish-and-chip shop proprietor and greengrocer. Especially considering they were (by the time I knew them, at least) three of the least romantic-looking people imaginable, unless trolls are considered romantic. Both Mr and Mrs Tom were about four-foot-nothing, and almost as wide (although no one ever got to corroborate it, we imagined they must have slept diagonally); while Nick, not much taller than the other two, was almost completely covered in a thick coat of coarse black hair, up to and including hands, but excluding head, which was shiny, pointed and, in stark contrast to the rest of him, totally bald. Even with his shirt done up to the collar it looked like a couple of furry creatures were trying to escape out the top, front and back.

Despite these physical shortcomings, however, they still managed to radiate a certain faded, soft afterglow, faint radio waves of their past great passions, requited and otherwise, in which you could occasionally discern the fire in which their younger hearts must have been forged. And they were, besides, always there. Two points of a triangle, our own house being the third.

We were forever running out of something or other, and I would be despatched to Tom's to get it, sneaking a furtive Turkish Delight whenever I thought I could get away with it, stuffing it in my mouth whole and choking it down before I got back. And Nick's, apart from the dubious appeal of his re-fried fish, always had a couple of pinball machines which were irresistible to a young boy with change in his pocket.

I would stand at a machine, barely able to see over the top, my arms stretched wide in a loving hug in order to reach the flipper buttons, and flip madly at that shiny steel ball as if my life depended on it. And nothing was more wonderful than those few occasions when I would happen upon a visit by the pinball mechanic, and get to peer inside the belly of one of those beautiful, mysterious, electronic beasts. And then, just before he closed it up again, with the slightest flick of a button he would bring up a dozen free games, and give them to me. 'There you go, kid,' he would say, simply, but he would never know how much it meant to me, those twelve free games on a pinball machine, and as I played them down (it probably didn't take very long, but time seemed to stand still for me then) I was in heaven, and have never been happier.

And whenever I went in, Nick would ask the same questions.

'How's your mother?' he would say.

'Good.'

'How's your father?'

'Good.'

'How's Ray?'

'Good.'

'How's Truman?'

'Good.'

'How's school?'

'Not bad.'

He would sit in his creaky old wicker chair while his fish fried up to nothing in one of the huge vats of boiling oil that teenagers used to flick cigarette butts into when he wasn't looking, and ask me endless questions about nothing, or seemingly nothing, and I would answer 'Yes' or 'No' or 'Good' or 'Not bad' and sometimes try to imagine Mrs Tom as Mrs Nick, and visualise her sitting there next to her husband, the fish-and-chip shop owner, perhaps in her own creaky old wicker chair, instead of next door in the greengrocer's with her greengrocer husband, and sense, although I couldn't really understand it, something of the mysterious undercurrents of this life, the forces that push and pull us this way or that, and sometimes even drag us under.

He was sitting there the last time I saw him, too, fish still frying away in one of the vats. The Kelly twins, Ronald and Donald, were standing there looking at him. They were waiting to order. I stood next to them, waiting to order too, and the three of us just looked at old Nick slumped there in his creaky old wicker chair, slack-jawed and silent.

'I think he's dead,' said Ronald, or perhaps Donald.

'I think you're right,' said the other one.

And that, as far as our fish and chips went, was that.

40

'Son of bitch, shit.'

———

David Hume, a Scottish philosopher who's been dead for over two hundred years, never, ever, as far as I know, said, 'Son of bitch, shit.' Certainly he didn't say it in any of his books, although it's possible he may have said it, or something similar, when his first one, *Treatise of Human Nature*, didn't quite crank up the sales he'd been hoping for. What he did say, however, was that although all our actions are the result, to a certain extent at least, of other, prior, actions – that is, of cause and effect – they aren't only the result of this.

He also factored in a healthy dollop of free will, the same thing Sartre was so keen on a couple of centuries later when he wasn't getting off with Simone de Beauvoir or some other French floozy. This mixture of causation and free will subsequently became known as compatibilism, a catchy little name which is probably more likely to pop up on the cover of *Marie-Claire* than anywhere else, but which, nonetheless, leads me to Robin Williams.

———

I once sold him a 20p postcard of James Bond, and although I wasn't expecting him to, he didn't say anything even remotely funny. He just shuffled up to me, gave me the money, mumbled an almost inaudible 'Thanks,' and shuffled off again, all without once taking his eyes off the ground, then walked into a wall. I wasn't going to, but perhaps he thought I looked like the kind of person who would say 'Na-nu, na-nu' if given half a chance, and he just wanted to avoid the embarrassment of having to tell me I was a knob if I did.

———

Following this close encounter with celebrity, and obeying the dictates of cause and effect, on the way home that night I popped into my local video store with the intention of renting *Moscow on the Hudson*, but it was out. So, taking my free will for a leisurely amble, rather than a cross-country sprint, I rented *Good Morning, Vietnam* instead.

———

In one scene Robin Williams's character inadvertently teaches the English class of the girl he hopes to cop off with the same exclamation that as far as I know David Hume never used except possibly in relation to his first book's disappointing sales, and watching it that night, eating a Pot Noodle washed down with a can of Sainsbury's own-brand beer, I thought teaching might be a fun thing to do (which, compared to washing down a Pot Noodle with a can of Sainsbury's own-brand beer,

I guess it was), and that, as far as just about everything else is concerned, was that.

———

The most useful thing I learned on my teacher-training course was never to hand out a worksheet before explaining what you wanted your students to do with it unless you particularly wanted to shout and bang on the table to get their attention again in order to tell them what they were supposed to do with the worksheet which you'd just given them before telling them what you wanted them to do with it in the first place. The most interesting thing was that Captain Kirk's voice-over at the beginning of *Star Trek* contains probably the world's most famous split infinitive:

  'To boldly go . . .'

41

Strolling to the tube station one day after class, my mind
still reeling with defining and non-defining relative
clauses, I heard a screech, and looking up had my first
and last glimpse of the still fluffy Fluffy as she hurtled
towards me out of a clear blue sky.

Sometimes things do.

———

Like the German fighter pilot who was shot down and,
fortunately for him, just managed to bail out in time,
only to then have his chute, unfortunately for him, refuse
to open. He subsequently spent the next, and last, eight
and a half seconds of his life unhappily hurtling towards
my father out of just such a clear sky. My father, who
only moments before had been standing on a hillside,
gazing rapturously skywards at the deadly dogfight
unfolding above him, not believing his luck at seeing
what he was seeing, now literally couldn't believe what
he was seeing. The pilot really did appear to be heading
straight for him, and not only did he appear to be
heading straight for him, but there appeared to be something crouched on his back, riding him almost, the para-
chute harness gripped in one hand, a long curved scythe
in the other.

He was nine years old and, like most nine-year-olds,

had never experienced death, much less seen him. He stood rooted to the spot, mesmerised. It could easily have been the end of him, as it looked pretty certain to be the end of the hapless pilot, but it wasn't. He obviously still had things to do, like grow up, and meet my mother, and propose until she said yes, and beget three children, myself included.

At the last moment, almost, he snapped out of it, diving clear just in time not to be pancaked. The pilot, whether he had things to do or not, hit the ground, not ten feet away, with a loud, flat, ground-shuddering *Slap*.

In movies and on TV people are always saying things like, 'Listen' and 'We have to talk' before delivering bad news or saying anything important to another character, more for the audience's benefit, I suspect, than in any attempt at replicating how people actually speak. They want to grab our attention, to let us know the characters are going to stop twittering on about nothing for a couple of minutes, and actually say something interesting, or at least relevant to the plot. Then, à la Pavlov's dog, our ears (if not necessarily our saliva glands) prick up, and we tune in long enough to be fed another tasty little morsel of essential information.

Sitting in the park a couple of weeks after kissing Cherry on Brighton beach I had something to tell her that was not only extremely relevant to our own particular plot, but could even be classified as that most breathlessly advertised film gimmick: the twist.

It too, like Fluffy and Dad's German pilot, was to appear out of a seemingly clear sky.

Unfortunately, in our case, Cherry never saw it coming.

Of course I'd had the previous two weeks to bring it up, but somehow I hadn't quite managed to get round to it. I'd meant to, naturally, but it was the kind of thing that's notoriously difficult to work into general conversation. Besides, looked at a certain way, it was all just a little misunderstanding. More specifically, a little misunderstanding concerning whether I did, or didn't, presently have a girlfriend. Obviously I did (two if you count Cherry), whereas Cherry herself was under the distinct impression I didn't.

I didn't say 'Listen' because that's what I said in class before switching on a tape for a listening exercise. 'OK, everyone. Hair back. Fingers in ears. Swizzle. Fingers out. No, you don't need to sniff them. Now, listen'; and I didn't say we had to talk, because we were already talking.

Instead, I said this:

'I've got something to tell you.'

———

It was no big deal, and she took it pretty well, considering. Considering I had lied to her and deceived her and exploited her naivety and trusting nature as well as my position of authority as her teacher and therefore someone she should have been able to trust and believe when they said their girlfriend had just left them for another woman. Of course I never imagined she would take it seriously, and it wasn't as if I told her expressly to get her to into bed, which wouldn't happen for another couple of months anyway. I told the whole class in the course of a lesson to demonstrate a grammar point, present perfect for present result of past activity.

'So what am I doing? Yes, I'm crying. But why am I crying?'

'Toothache?' someone volunteered.

'No. Look at these teeth. They're perfect!'

'You think you're going to die?' someone else said.

'You think a little thing like death could make me cry? I laugh in the face of death every day.'

'You're unhappy?'

'Of course I'm unhappy. Naturally I'm unhappy. Look at me. I'm crying my eyes out like a baby. But why I'm crying, why I'm unhappy, is because my girlfriend – the *bitch*! – has left me.'

'Really?' gasped my class, almost as one.

It was a routine. Teaching's like that. Half the time it's like performing bad stand-up comedy.

'And you know what the worst part is? . . . She left me for another woman.'

They laughed right on cue, always did, every time.

'And so I'm unhappy now – present result – because she left me last week – past activity. So if we're still being affected now by something that happened in the past we use the present perfect. Got it?'

'Got it.'

'My God, I'm good.'

42

One lunchtime, not long before I jokingly told my students my girlfriend had left me for another woman, I popped back to class to get something and accidentally surprised Cherry absorbed in a Korean translation of D. H. Lawrence's *Women In Love*. Apparently it was one of her favourite books, but not only that, it turned out she'd read just about everyone else who'd ever knocked out a Penguin classic as well, read Chaucer for fun and never left home without a copy of Shakepeare's sonnets. She was completely potty about literature and poetry. In fact, I'd never met anyone so passionate about books before, and never met a Korean even remotely interested in them. She was easily the most beautiful student I'd ever taught, but this was the first sign of her real uniqueness. She looked like a Japanese Manga cartoonist's wet dream, *and* she read Goethe.

I would often hear other students talking about her, particularly the Koreans. No doubt they regarded her as something of a stuck-up princess, which I guess she was, but she really was almost like a different species. The way she dressed, her attitude, the way she moved, talked, laughed, the rarefied atmosphere of privilege which clung to her, her sheer devil-may-care hauteur. She was cold, aloof and totally indifferent to anyone or anything she didn't like, and she couldn't be flattered. When she walked past, all eyes were on her, but she seemed, genuinely, not even to notice.

I, on the other hand, couldn't help it.

Being with her was my first experience of the strange and powerful effect the truly beautiful can have on the populace at large, and not from my more usual rubbernecking perspective looking on, but from the first-hand reflected glare of that intense and constant spotlight itself.

At first I would catch people's eyes, not jealously, or threateningly, or challengingly, but simply in recognition that I knew they were checking out my girlfriend (with perhaps a tacit acknowledgement that if I'd been in their position I'd be doing exactly the same thing), but I soon took my cue from Cherry herself, and acted as if I weren't even aware of their existence, much less their ardent and obvious attentions, although, as I say, I was acting.

To be honest, I enjoyed it.

———

Occasionally, very, very occasionally, usually when I see a new Calvin Klein advertisement, I wish I was good-looking. Really good-looking. Impossibly good-looking. Calvin Klein good-looking. Of course it soon passes, in fact in about the time it takes me to turn the page, or look away from the billboard, but for that moment or two in which I imagine myself the possessor of perfect beauty, sauntering around in that impossibly toned, buffed body, gazing out of those smouldering, dreamy eyes set above those perfectly proportioned features, it does seem important, terribly important, to be beautiful.

Thankfully the rest of the time I'm reasonably content

to make my way through life looking exactly like me – no Brad Pitt, but not Quasimodo either.

In other words, or rather in Popeye's words, 'I yam what I yam!'

But what was I, and what was it that Cherry (or Cassie for that matter) saw in me, apart from the obvious, and unremarkable, surface? As far as eligible bachelors went, I was neither, and yet I had managed to land, and almost by accident at that, the kind of catch that you want to both eat and mount, and at the same time set free again because you know you're not worthy of having landed it in the first place.

The truth is, I was at the right place at the right time, or maybe even at the wrong place at the wrong time, when Cherry found herself washed up and disoriented on my little patch of beach, nothing but the odd piece of flotsam and jetsam still swirling about in the violent whirlpool left by her recently self-torpedoed way of life.

———

She told me later that when she first saw me, and in particular the small tuft of chest hair peeking out at my collar, she imagined I must be covered, ape-like, in a thick coat of body hair. I'm not, but our subsequent relationship was all the more surprising as she had an almost pathological horror of hirsuteness. She once even ended a friendship when the friend in question turned up one day wearing shorts, thus exposing his until then undisclosed hairy legs. He promised never to wear shorts again, but it was no good. Once she knew what horrors lurked up his trouser legs, she would have been unable to put it out of her mind when she saw him, or even talked to him on the phone, so that, as far as her hairy-legged ex-friend was concerned, was that.

———

One day, out of the blue, her presumably unhairy ex-fiancé just turned up, or rather, didn't so much just turn up as turn up after spending over a year single-mindedly, obsessively even, tracking her down. The reason he'd been tracking her down, of course, and what he wanted now that he'd found her, was obvious.

He wanted her back.

'Guess what?' she asked me.

'What?'

'My ex-fiancé called me.'

She always called him her 'ex-fiancé', never by his name. I still don't know it.

'You're kidding? How did he know where you were? How did he get the number?'

'I don't know.'

'Is he OK? Are you OK?'

'Yeah, I'm OK. But I don't think he's OK,' she said.

'Why? What do you mean?'

'He's here.'

'Here? Where here?'

'London.'

'How did he know you were in London?'

'I don't know.'

'What does he want?' I asked, but of course I already knew. What does anyone want who has gone to so much trouble to find someone who has gone to an equal amount of trouble not to be found?

'Me.'

Yes, her.

He wanted her back.

Who wouldn't?

He wanted her back despite the pain and humiliation she'd caused him. He wanted her back despite the fact he'd be a laughing stock. He wanted her back despite the damage it would cause to his relationship with his family. He wanted her back even if she didn't love him any more, even if she'd found someone else, even if she were no longer the innocent, wide-eyed virgin she'd been, even if she was in love with me, belonged to me.

———

This sudden appearance of his couldn't have come at a worse time for me, or a better time for him. Our relationship had reached another one of its regular impasses, only worse. We had arrived at that point where whatever comfort or hope or belief in a future, our future, that could possibly be wrung from the already pretty unconvincing phrase 'Don't worry, everything will be OK' was well and truly exhausted, bankrupt, wrung dry. I had flogged it to a threadbare rag of meaningless words, the utterance of which now merely served to throw into stark relief the hollowness and empty promise behind them. Once upon a time she had believed every word I told her, but these words, these simple words intended to fortify her, to keep her going (or to keep her hanging on) had become, every time I mouthed them, so much salt scattered over her already flayed heart. I was quite accomplished at investing things I didn't believe in with the stamp of truth, and even things I wanted to believe in, or didn't know whether I believed in or not, but we had now reached a place where it was kinder to promise nothing, and for her to expect the same.

So, as I say, it couldn't have come at a worse time for me, or a better one for him. If ever the conditions were ripe to sweep her, if not exactly off her feet, at least back into a first-class seat on the next plane to Seoul (a la carte menu in hand), then this was it.

He had descended from the skies, literally, offering, triumphantly yet modestly, almost divine forgiveness, reconciliation and reunion, while I, clapped-out and grounded, with a baggage hold full of superannuated promises, offered exactly bugger-all.

———

Of course that's when I should have let her go. It was so obviously the right thing to do. So she didn't love him? So she loved me? He would turn himself inside out to make her happy, whereas I didn't even know what I wanted, or who I wanted, or rather who I wanted the most, and had almost managed, single-handedly, to wipe the smile from her soul.

Naturally, I convinced her to stay.

———

So that he'd finally and once and for all put her behind him and get on with his life she told him she was engaged, shortly to be married, and, in a lie so breathtakingly bald-faced it made the other two appear minor tweakings of the truth by comparison, nothing less than blissfully happy, and so he wished her a beautiful new life, and left the next day.

43

I was debating whether to call Cherry or not when there was a call for me and it was her and in an uncharacteristic burst of honesty I told her that I had just been trying to decide if I should call her or not.

'Why?' she asked. 'Don't you want to talk to me?'

'You told me not to call you. I didn't know whether I should or not.'

'What do you think?' she asked me.

'I don't know,' I told her, lamely.

'It makes me angry when you call and it makes me angry when you don't call. So it doesn't matter what you do. Up to you.'

'OK,' I said.

'Yeah, everything is OK. Everything is perfect.'

Thus far into the conversation I was already pretty sure that not calling her would have been the best decision, as would have been not taking her call, or even, in that misguided burst of honesty, telling her that I had been trying to decide whether I should call or not.

'So, what have you been doing?' I asked.

'Nothing.'

'Nothing?'

'Like usual. Nothing special. Nothing.'

Then she didn't say anything, and as I had exactly

nothing to say, or at least nothing except what I'd already said a thousand times before, I said the last thing I should have said.

'Can I see you?'

'Why? What's the point?'

And then, because I'd already said the last thing I should have said, I said the next but last.

'I miss you.'

She thought this was much funnier than it was, and laughed a short, hard laugh, the kind, I realised with a shock, she would have been incapable of a year before. 'Oh, really?' she said. 'Thank you very much.'

And then I really outdid myself.

'I want to see you because I miss you and I love you,' I told her, and even as I was telling her this, the three most important things in her life, I was making a paper clip chain from the dish of paper clips on the desk. I had the phone wedged under my chin and was idly looping them together.

There was a long silence.

'Don't say that. You can't say that,' she said softly.

'But it's true,' I told her.

Bastard!

'Don't say anything.'

'So will I come round?'

Heel!

'If you want.'

'So I'll see you after school?'

Wanker!

'OK.'

'OK, I'll see you then.'

Worm!

Before I could hang up, she asked quickly, 'What time?'

'I don't know. After school. As soon as I can.'

'OK . . . Bye.'

———

'Guess what?'

'What?'

'I think maybe I'm pregnant.'

Oh, great big fat fuck!

———

She took a second test to be sure, and then we went to a doctor so she could have a blood test, to be absolutely sure, and after each test, the home pregnancy tests, then the blood test, I couldn't help feeling there must be some kind of mistake, that she couldn't possibly be pregnant. It was too melodramatic, too ironic, too grown-up, but most of all it was too unreal. I watched myself go through the same motions I'd seen again and again in movies and on TV, those same old clichés. A baby! A sudden, unexpected baby! How will the characters react? Will the father-to-be be pleased? Will he whoop and holler and leap about on the furniture? Or will he be bewildered, shocked? Maybe at first he'll be stony-faced, emotionless, and the mother-to-be will look on anxiously, studying his face for any flicker of what he might be thinking, the suspense building, before he suddenly grabs her up in his arms, twirling her round. 'I'm going to be a father!' he cries, joyously, while the girl says sensibly as she's either being tossed in the air like a salad or crushed like a walnut, 'Careful, darling – remember the baby.' Or then again he might be angry, accusatory. It's all her fault, her responsibility. What was she thinking anyway? They can't have a baby now. It couldn't be worse timing. What about his career? His plans? What about his carefree do-whatever-the-hell-he-likes-when-ever-he-likes swinging lifestyle?

Holy crap, what about my girlfriend?

44

'She's pregnant,' I said.

'Who is?' asked Raymond.

'Cherry.'

'Ah! Can I take it that as you're not handing out cigars, plus you look like you might crap in your pants at any moment, this is less than thrilling news?'

'You can, and I am. Crapping my pants, I mean.'

'Are you sure?'

'That I'm crapping my pants?'

'That she's pregnant?'

'Sure. Double sure. Triple sure. One hundred percent totally triple sure.'

'That's pretty sure. So what are you going to do?'

'What do you mean?'

'What do you mean, what do you mean? I mean what are you going to do about it?'

The third person pronoun hit me like a sledgehammer.

'"It"?' I repeated, wonderingly. 'Huh. That's just what it is, isn't it? An "it". I've created an "it". "It" lives. Well, we can't have it, obviously. I'm too young to have a baby "it".'

'You're thirty-six, Ben.'

'That's what I mean. I'm too young. I can't have a baby now. I'd have to start working hard to buy it stuff. And save for the future. And act responsibly. And put it first. And everywhere I went, every time I left the house, I'd have to pack as much stuff as if I were going in search of Dr-fucking-Livingstone. And I'd have to act interested, and doting, and paternal, and socialise with other people with kids, and all we'd ever do is talk about kids, and it would always be there, not just for a while, but forever, until I die. And then, what would be even worse, what if I turned into one of those people who don't even realise what they're doing, what they've become, who go around telling other, childless, happy people, that it's the best thing that's ever happened to them. And what if – as I suspect it is – that isn't just something that people with kids go around telling people without kids in a pathetic attempt to make their lives seem less desperate and miserable, but what if they actually *believe* it? What if I become one of them? A pod person – outwardly me, but inwardly one of them. I don't want to be one of them, Ray. I don't want to be a pod person.'

And then Ray, practical and matter-of-fact as ever, voiced the thought that made all these other thoughts, as horrifying as they undoubtedly were, by comparison seem like the rather pleasant side-effects of a natural and joyous blessing.

'And it might be quite awkward breaking the news to Cassie, too,' he said.

———

There's bad timing, and then there's that which transcends bad timing, and then there was this. Of course I mouthed the usual assurances and empty promises – 'It'll be OK, We'll do whatever you want, I'd love to have a baby with you one day, If everything weren't so crazy,' etc. – which, interestingly and for the first time in my life, as I reeled them off, I actually felt, just as in the evergreen expression, turn to ashes in my mouth.

But there was never any real doubt about what we were going to do.

I guess I made sure of that.

Was there guilt? Not about the abortion, no, but for her? Yes, because I knew I was damaging her and that she had and would forgive me anything. She was a thousand times better than me and I knew it and she knew it but she didn't care because she loved me with every fibre of her body and I recklessly impregnated her and even though the choice was ultimately hers I was happy and could, besides, and with only a word, have made her do whatever I wanted.

'I love you,' I told her, and wished I had even enough conviction left to hate myself.

45

I was sitting on the toilet reading a magazine when Cassie just walked in, not by accident either, as can sometimes happen, but intentionally, and obviously with something on her mind. No. 1s could be communal, you could clean your teeth while the other person was peeing, or have a shower, or a bath, or even just a chat, but No. 2s were strictly private affairs. I therefore looked up in some surprise at this unexpected intrusion, but she just stood there, slightly distracted, and then she said, 'This isn't working.'

'What isn't?' I asked.

'This. Us. Everything,' she said, simply. 'Our relationship. It's just not working.'

To say I was taken aback would be akin to saying Michelangelo's *David* is a piece of rock.

I simply stared at her in disbelief.

'What do you mean it's not working?'

'I mean it's not working,' she clarified, less than helpfully.

'Of course it's working,' I said. 'It's working fine.'

'No it isn't, Benton. It's a disaster. A total, unadulterated, fucked-up disaster,' she clarified further, more helpfully this time.

'Are you crazy? How can you say that? We've got a great relationship. It's perfect! It's wonderful! It couldn't be better!'

'No we haven't. You may think we have, but we haven't. What we've actually got is a horrible, mangled, train wreck of a disaster. We're slowly sucking the life out of each other. We're nothing but a couple of vampires.'

'What are you talking about? How can you compare us to vampires? Jesus! What do you mean we're nothing but a couple of vampires? That's crazy!'

'We're no good for each other, Ben.'

'How can you say that? How can you stand there and say we're no good for each other? We're great for each other! We're perfect for each other!'

'Are we?'

'Of course we are. We love each other.'

'Do we?'

'What d'you mean, do we? Of course we do. We're crazy about each other. We adore each other.'

'But do we really, Ben? I mean really? If we loved each other – I mean *really* loved each other – would I wake up in the middle of the night and feel like suffocating you with my pillow?'

'What?'

'Don't tell me you don't feel the same way?'

'Of course I don't feel the same way. Are you insane? Why would I want to suffocate you? I love you.'

And then she said, although not one of the top-ranking most stupid things I'd ever heard anyone say in my life, something at least worthy of an honourable mention.

'We all kill the thing we love.'

I stared at her even harder than I had been staring at her before, which was already quite hard.

'What the fuck does that mean?' I said.

'It doesn't matter. Anyway, I think you should leave.'

'You think I should leave?'

'I think it would be best.'

'What do you mean, exactly – leave?'

'Move out. And I think you should do it as soon as possible.'

And it was over – we were over – just like that.

Or almost over.

She popped her head back round the door. 'And don't forget to use the air freshener when you're done,' she added. 'It really smells in here.'

———

She hadn't discovered any incriminating notes, or letters, or photos; no lipstick stains on my collar, or condoms in my wallet; she hadn't found a scrap of paper with a strange telephone number on it, but no name, and called it; she hadn't, in the end, caught me in the act, or been told by someone who had; she hadn't been suspiciously hung up on when she answered the phone, or found scratch marks on my back; she hadn't caught me out in a lie, or smelling of someone else's perfume, or read any suspicious text messages; I hadn't been buying new underwear, or started wearing cologne; I hadn't suddenly started working late, or irregular hours, or been acting aloof, or cold, or distant; I hadn't called her by the wrong name, or some cute new nickname; she hadn't hired a private detective, or bought one of those do-it-yourself kits where you can test your suspected love rat's knickers for traces of spunk, or whatever it is you test for; she hadn't even so much as suspected, although I was sometimes amazed she hadn't. She was simply sick of me, and I really couldn't blame her.

After she'd closed the door on me, on us, I just sat there, I don't know how long, unable to breathe almost. It felt like I'd been stabbed in the heart, which was funny, because who'd have guessed I even had one.

46

We were due at the clinic at three o'clock, but we weren't going to go, not now. We were going to have the baby. It was my turn to suddenly grab my girl up in my arms and spin her round, crying joyously, 'Everything's going to be OK! Really OK! I've made up my mind, or rather my mind's been made up for me, but it doesn't matter! I'm going to start afresh! No more cheating, or lying, or sneaking around. I'm going to be a decent person! I'm going to be a father!' But when I got to Cherry's flat, and rang the bell, there was no answer. I looked at my watch. She should've been there, getting ready. I called her mobile, standing there outside her building, barely able to contain myself. I wanted to shout it out. 'I'm a new person! And I'm going to be a better person! I'm going to grab hold of life by the proverbials, and live it, really live it! No more wasting time! No more going through the motions! Today, ladies and gentlemen of the world, fellow human beings of this beautiful planet, is the day the rest of my life begins!'

'Hello?' she said.

'It's me, where are you?' I asked, before it went dead.

I called straight back, but she'd turned it off, and all at once it hit me. I didn't have hold of life by the balls, nor was I going to.

It had me by mine.

———

I don't know how long it took me to get there, except that the taxi I'd leapt into was too slow, and I'd jumped out again, and run, and run, not like a man possessed, but actually possessed, but she'd already gone in by the time I burst through the door into the startled waiting room full of couples, and girls with their mothers, or girlfriends, and girls all alone, but none of them Cherry. Maybe I should have called reception and asked to talk to her, and if she wouldn't come to the phone, told them something, made up some story to stop them letting her go through with it. She wasn't responsible for her actions. She was on anti-depressants. She was an illegal immigrant. She wasn't really pregnant. Or simply, she was having my baby. *Our* baby. But I didn't think of it, and I didn't have the number, and it wouldn't have done any good anyway.

'You have to let me see her,' I told the receptionist.

'I'm sorry, sir. She's already been put under.'

'Please,' I begged. '*Please*!'

'I'm sorry,' she said, placing her hand on mine where it sat trembling on the top of the desk. 'It's too late.'

———

She was sitting wearing a white robe much too big for her. There were probably another nine or ten women, or girls, also wearing robes, either waiting for someone, with someone, or else going through it by themselves. Some were with their boyfriends, or husbands, a girlfriend or sister, and one was with her mother.

Cherry looked like a child. Her robe enveloped her.

Only her face and hands were visible. Her face was pale and she was holding a plastic cup of tea, but not drinking it. No two girls were sitting within ten feet of each other. Little pockets of misery and relief. I looked at her and thought she had never looked so beautiful or that I had ever loved her so much and I wanted to cry. Then she saw me but her face was like a mask. I went over and sat down beside her and held her but it felt like I had an armful of robe and nothing else. She had disappeared inside it.

'Are you OK?'

She answered mechanically.

'I'm fine.'

'How's the tea?'

'Not bad.'

'How do you feel?'

'Fine.'

I held her hand, which was tiny, like the hand of a toy, or a doll. I remembered the first time I'd held it, or rather she held mine. She'd wanted to read my palm, and held my hand in hers while she studied it thoughtfully, occasionally tracing along a crease with a slim, delicate finger. She wasn't being provocative, or coming on to me – I was her teacher, for God's sake, and she wouldn't have known how even if she'd wanted to. She genuinely believed in fate, and fortune-tellers, and wanted to show me what wonderful things awaited me.

I was to have a long life (of course), and to marry (naturally), and have kids (she wasn't sure how many, either two or five), and I would be successful, and happy, and die (at a ripe old age) in my bed.

Perfect!

———

Her own life, however, had taken a turn she could never have imagined when she decided to turn her back on everything she'd known, risk everything, and start again fresh – fresh as spring! Fresh as a daisy! 'Fresh!' she would say, stepping out of the bathroom after taking a shower, wrapped up in a towel, her hair piled up in another like a turban. She was the cleanest person I had ever known. She would wash her clothes first by hand, and then by machine. She would clean her teeth five times a day, and when she smoked the occasional cigarette, she would only do it in the bathroom, with the window open. Then she would put the butt (only ever half smoked) in a sealable plastic bag, before disposing of it in the bin. And then she would spray air freshener and clean her teeth again. Fresh! She was that blast of fresh air we hear so much about, that blows away cobwebs, and mustiness, and stale, dead air. For a while it had filled my lungs, I was high on it like pure oxygen, but she only had so much to give, and all I did was suck, suck, suck, until she was dry, empty, all out, and this was all that was left, this small, cold, lifeless hand in mine.

'What happens next?' I asked.

'I have to go to the toilet, then see the doctor to make sure everything's OK.'

'It won't be long now,' the woman at the checkout desk told us, and added, to me, 'You've got a very beautiful girlfriend. She should be a model.'

Ten minutes later it was Cherry's turn and she went to the toilet before being examined by the doctor for bleeding.

47

There were women and men, half a dozen of them, with placards, and some of them I vaguely noticed had books in their hands – thick, black, leather-bound books. At first it didn't register what they were doing. I could see that their mouths were moving, and their faces were angry, but it felt like we'd stepped outside into a vacuum. They were shouting – apparently at us, but why? Then I looked at their placards, their horrible, homemade placards with blown-up pictures of aborted foetuses on them, and their voices suddenly crashed over me like a wave.

'Repent!'

'Pray for the soul of your dead baby!'

'Thou shalt not kill!'

I wasn't angry at first, just stunned. Stunned that they could do this. Stunned at their cruelty, their arrogance, their stupidity, their ignorance, their complete lack of humanity, feeling, heart, sympathy, compassion and any semblance of decency; the sheer depravity of their minds, their black evil souls, their self-righteous, filth-spouting, may-they-burn-in-hell Godless bastardry, and then I was angry.

'Why don't you all fuck off and die,' I told them.

'Repent for the unborn soul you've sent to purgatory!'

'Go home and think about your innocent murdered baby, and pray for forgiveness!'

I'd stopped, which, for no other reason than for Cherry, I shouldn't have done. And inside me an almost nuclear fusion of anger was taking place, my own little Fat Boy of fury, and for the first and only time in my life I wanted to kill, was capable of killing.

And then I just went Boom!

I don't know what I said or did, but when the dazzling, blinding flash of my rage cleared, and I could see again, think again, the protesting pro-lifers were scattered like ten pins. There were smashed placards, torn Bibles, ripped clothing, scratch marks, bite marks, bloody noses. Whatever had happened, I'd obviously been indiscriminate as far as sex, and given the women as good as I gave the men. There was sobbing from the former and abuse from the latter.

My own clothes were ripped and torn, and I could taste blood – probably a busted lip. My knuckles were grazed, and there were scratch marks and a couple of bite marks on my arms, which, I guessed later, were probably done in trying to unclasp my hands from one of their miserable throats. The back of my head was hurt too, although I couldn't feel it yet, where, touching it gingerly an hour later, sitting on a park bench in Kensington Gardens, I thought (with a smile) someone might have hit me with a Bible.

I felt dazed.

My monumental fury was extinguished, had burned itself out in a white-hot flash and left me drained, empty, and lifeless. I looked at Cherry and felt ashamed, ashamed for what she'd gone through, what I'd put her through, what she must have felt, arriving at the clinic by herself and having to make her way through those, whatever they believed in, and no matter how strongly they believed it, unpardonable pricks.

But it was all my fault, my doing, not theirs, not anyone's, and nothing, not beating people up, not venting my spleen, not loving her, or needing her, or wanting to make it all up to her, somehow, some way, could change that, or make things one jot better.

I was the villain of the piece.

I was the bad guy.

'I'm sorry,' I said. 'I'm sorry.'

She was crying, not violently, or hysterically, but quietly, effortlessly, as though it was all she had left. She stood there, looking at me, and the tears simply fell from those beautiful, wounded, never-to-be-forgotten eyes.

And then she said the two most painful words, perhaps, one human being can say to another.

'It's over.'

48

I don't know how long I'd been sitting there before I realised the back of my head was sore and touched it gingerly, smiling to myself at the thought that one of those sons of bitches must have hit me with a Bible, or more probably, by the feel of it, a placard. It was getting late, and the park was already nearly empty. It was also cold, although I knew this more by my icy puffs of breath than anything else. The last few stragglers making their way home were all wrapped up in coats and jackets, and I remembered I'd started out the day wearing one myself. I guessed I must have lost it somewhere along the way, in the taxi, or throwing it away in my mad dash to the clinic, or maybe I'd left it at the clinic itself. I loved that jacket, too. Vintage leather, comfortably beat up and lived in. I'd bought it years ago, with Cassie. She'd spotted it and instantly said, 'Oh, this is so you!' And I loved it immediately, but felt sure it wouldn't fit, because it was perfect, and cheap, and I thought the arms would be too short for sure, not because I had particularly long arms, but because funky people in the seventies, judging by the clothes that have survived, were so stumpy. But the sleeves weren't too short, and it fitted perfectly, and I bought it, and had worn it through everything, and even nearly lost it a couple of times, once in a pub, when I was pissed, and got halfway home before I realised and had to go back for it, and once when I left it on a bus, but jumped back on at the last minute to find another passenger already trying it on, the bastard.

Anyway, it was gone now, or maybe not. I might be lucky and have left it at the clinic. This made me laugh, the thought of going back there. The thought of those daft picketers, bruised and bandaged, their placards stuck back together with glue and Sellotape (up half the night doing that, they would be). I'd enjoy the looks on their faces when they saw me – as long as they hadn't brought reinforcements, or armed themselves heavily. And then, not unnaturally, I thought of the look on Cherry's face, and I didn't feel like laughing any more, or crying. I just felt empty.

And then I noticed I had company.

'Hello, little fella.'

It was a hedgehog, something I'd never actually seen before, except for the occasional squashed one by the side of the road. It had waddled up quite close to me, and just stood there, kind of stretching out its neck and mewling at me. It was almost as if the little guy had sensed I was a bit down, and had come over to sympathise, one prickly pear to another. 'Whatever's up with you,' he seemed to be saying, 'can't be worse than a steady diet of worms for the rest of your life.'

Of course I realised hedgehogs could see about as well as bats (or was I thinking of moles?), and that in the failing light he probably couldn't even see me, or had mistaken me for someone else, but as far as consolation or company went, he was about all I was going to get.

'Read any good books lately?' I asked him, but he hadn't. Hadn't seen any good movies either, or even bad ones. Turned out he was a hedgehog of simple tastes. He liked snuffling about, digging a bit, and worms. That was it really.

Then, during a longer than usual lull in the conversation, I noticed it was late and the park deserted, and for the first time I suddenly realised I was cold.

'Well, it's been nice chatting with you,' I said, shivering and getting up. 'Enjoy those worms.'

I sensed it before I saw it, or even heard it, and when I turned around it was nearly on us. I think it was a mastiff of some denomination, but I'm not sure which, or even if they come in different types. Whatever it was, it was huge, coming at us out of the gloom like something out of the Baskervilles, and I didn't like the way it was eyeballing my new little friend.

'Shoo!' I cried. 'Shoo!'

It paid me about as much attention as two hundred pounds of slavering dog ought to have paid me, and little Mr Tiggy Winkle (I couldn't think of him as a Mrs) was clearly on the menu, or at least on the sporting curriculum. And the next instant, before I even knew what I'd done, I'd scooped him up to what I laughingly considered safety. I say laughingly considered safety because the beast, as I almost instantly thought of him, or her, or it, hardly appeared to notice, and just tried to run right up me to get at the poor mewling creature, which I desperately held at arm's length above my head.

'Fuck off! Fuck off!' I yelled at it, looking round frantically for its owner, assuming it had one and hadn't just sprung up from some portal from hell.

I've always loved dogs, and indeed animals in general, but this dog I loathed, loathed it with a passion, and I loathed its owner as well, wherever the fuck he was, and at the same time I was scared shitless, but I was damned if it was going to get this hedgehog. 'Get your own bloody hedgehog!' I yelled, fending it off desperately, and before I knew it, somehow, I had clambered up a tree.

My heart was pounding, but I was curiously exultant as well. The great beast might have been able to tear me limb from limb, to crush me in its jaws like a meringue, possibly even lick me to death, but I'd outsmarted it, outwitted it, outmanoeuvred it, or at least outclimbed it. It capered about the bottom of the tree, its huge, slobbery tongue lolling out, and I gave it the universally recognised sign of defiance and disdain, adding an, 'Up yours, Rover!' just for good measure. And then there was a loud, piercing whistle, the kind kids used to do in the toilets at school, when it would be so loud because of the confined space you'd have to cover your ears, and the great dumb mutt was off like a shot to its master, without so much as a second thought for us, its erstwhile prey.

I considered letting its owner have a mouthful, but the thought of berating an invisible person over his dog at night in the park from up a tree with a hedgehog was just silly, so I didn't. And after all, it was just being a dog, and its owner, at this time of night, and not unreasonably, must have thought they had the place pretty much to themselves, and couldn't have dreamed there was now a man stuck up a tree because he'd bought a wolfhound, or whatever it was, instead of a Pekinese. And now that I could think about things in those very rational terms, I realised something else.

I realised I really was stuck up a tree.

With a hedgehog, no less.

———

I didn't panic, that's the first thing I didn't do. Then I didn't shout out for help, although it might not have been such a bad plan. But for some reason I'd never really been comfortable with the whole shouting out for help idea, although I could see it had a lot going for it in certain situations, my present one included. Perhaps it was an overdeveloped sense of reserve, or reticence, or unwillingness to be seen to be vulnerable. After all, no one is quite so helpless as the person calling out for help. By then they've dropped all pretence of being able to get out of it – whatever it may be – by themselves. By the time they're shouting out for help they're well and truly up the proverbial creek without the proverbial paddle, and all they can do is sit back and hope to be rescued.

And so I didn't panic, and I didn't shout, although I was certainly in need of rescuing, and so was my hedgehog, but I did pull out my mobile and call the person Cassie and I had always said we would call if one or the other of us ever met with some freakish and totally unexpected accident, or found ourselves in a situation from which we were unable to extricate ourselves, such as being stuck up a tree, in a park, at night, with a wild, albeit sweet-natured animal for company.

I called my brother Ray.

———

'Hello?'

'You'll never believe where I am,' I told him.

'Benny-boy! Where have you been? I've been calling your place all day, and I don't know why you even bother with a mobile. You know you have to turn those things on, little brother?'

'I've been kind of busy –'

'Well, I've got news, fella. Some Hollywood fatcats have bought my book. They're going to make a film of *Adventures of a Rubber Duck*! Is that deranged or what? They want to get Tom Hanks to play the duck, or maybe beef it up a bit, add a few fights, a couple of car chases, and maybe get Tom Cruise, but I don't think he's got the range. What a hoot! It'll be a total fucking disaster.'

'Ray, can you come and get me?'

'What is it? Are you OK?'

'I've had a really strange day, Ray.'

'Where are you?'

And I told him.

'You won't believe this, but I'm already on my way there. My regular fare's only just this minute popped out of thin air, as he does. I've got the address right next to me. Palace Gates, Kensington Gardens.'

'Oh, shit, Ray. Oh, shit.'

'What is it, kid? Are you OK? I'll be there as quick as I can. I'm putting my foot to the floor. Hang on!'

———

But that's just what I couldn't do. My world was turned upside-down, and no matter how tightly I might hold on, you can only defy gravity for so long. And so my foot slipped, and I reached out, desperately, to steady myself with one hand, because I was still cradling my little friend in the other, and I missed, grabbed a handful of air. It threw me off balance, and with nothing to hold on to, I went over backwards, and landed with a dull, hard, unhealthy thump.

49

It knocks the wind out of me, and at first I just lie there trying to get as much of that back as I can. When I was a kid we used to call it 'winded', and it was a routine part of life. Kids were always getting the wind knocked out of them (not to mention the crap, or in the other direction, sense), playing football, or rugby, or British Bulldog, or even just copping a good hard punch in the breadbasket would do it. But it was years since I'd experienced it, and I'd forgotten that little rush of panic you get, when for those first few seconds you find your lungs so uncharacteristically empty of air.

Something else I hadn't had for years was a dead leg, those sudden, surprise attacks to the side of your leg by some bastard's knee, and you'd just crumple up. But as soon as you recovered you'd charge off, vengefully intent on returning the favour to the kid who just got you, or if you couldn't find him, some other kid would do.

Imagine what society would be like if we never grew out of stuff like that. There'd be politicians going about dead-legging each other, and husbands and wives giving each other Chinese burns, and people in offices kneeling down behind their colleagues while someone else started up a conversation with them about paper clips or something before suddenly giving them a little shove and over they'd go.

I give a little chuckle at that, so I must have got my wind back.

Actually, I'm quite comfortable, apart from what feels like a root stuck in my back. And I never imagined London could be so quiet, so peaceful. I can't hear so much as a car, or a voice. I could be deep in the remotest countryside somewhere except for the fact I know I'm not, I'm here, lying flat on my back at the foot of a tree, alone and unable to move in the middle of a thriving metropolis of seven-million-odd people.

Odd people.

Odd.

You know what's odd?

Three.

Three's the oddest number in the whole wide world.

Nothing beats it for oddness.

Not the Push-Me-Pull-You, and that was the oddest thing Dr Dolittle had ever seen.

Not the platypus.

Not the fact that *Titanic* is the most successful movie of all time.

Not modern-day Druids.

Not even the comb-over.

And nothing, absolutely nothing, is odder than that eternal geometric configuration, the triangle.

———

We both loved trains, Cassie and me, not in a trainspotting sense, but in a travelling on them to somewhere nice sense. Every so often we would pack a bag and head to Paddington, or Victoria, or Charing Cross, and decide, on the spot, where to go away for the weekend, depending on what trains were about to leave. It might be Whitby, or Windsor, or Eastbourne, or Stratford-upon-Avon, or anywhere else we could get to in a couple of hours, and sometimes the place would be great, and sometimes it wouldn't, but it didn't matter, we always had a ball, and we would take pictures of everything, our fish and chips, our room, a duck with a particularly expressive quack, and once, on fateful Brighton beach, our bare feet, lying on our backs with them stuck up in the air against a perfect blue sky.

I would never have believed feet could look so happy.

———

For a long time we had it stuck on the fridge, then we got a new fridge, and it disappeared for a while, but resurfaced with a lot of other bits and pieces that had also been stuck on it, or on top of it, and we both smiled at it again, remembering how happy we'd been, and Cassie finally put it in a frame, and it got moved from place to place, until I couldn't even say where it was exactly, although like so many other things, ticket stubs, theatre programmes, mix tapes we'd made one another, scribbled notes saying everything from 'I love you' to 'Just popped out for a pint of milk', birthday cards, anniversary cards, Valentine's Day cards, seashells we'd collected, a cornucopia of what anyone else except us would call so much crap, and which would be crap to anyone except us, it was still there, somewhere, embedded in its very own geological layer, prematurely fossilised now, a relic, but as representative of the relationship as anything else, I guess.

———

Cherry and I had our own relics too now. For a while, before things went bad, she used to get me to read her favourite poems aloud, and she'd record them on her small dictaphone, then listen to them at night, often drifting off to sleep to them.

I did a whole tapeful, tripping over words, giggling, sometimes feeling embarrassed, or self-conscious, sometimes slipping in the odd saucy ad lib (but she took her poetry seriously and would always make me do it again, reading the proper lines).

I must have recorded some of the finest, most beautiful, most profound lines ever written, immortal words that had, and do, and would continue to live and breathe and inspire as long as people care about things like living and breathing and being inspired.

Now that was funny.

That was hilarious.

———

I wonder what Georgia thought about lying out there in the snow. You hear about people's lives flashing before their eyes in that split second when they think they're about to die all the time, but does it really, I wonder? And what about when it takes a long time to die? Perhaps instead of flashing by, it just kind of meanders by, taking its time, unfolding itself like a leisurely tale told by somebody in no great hurry to get to the end, because, basically, they know it's the end.

I read somewhere that the most common last words recorded on planes' black boxes when they're about to crash are, 'Oh, shit!'

Understandable.

I wonder if she thought of us? Her and me. Our time together. Our lives together. Most of hers, and nearly half of mine now.

I wonder if she felt cold.

I don't.

I can't feel anything.

Oh, yes I can. I can feel my little friend.

I can feel him snuffling about on my chest.

I can feel his prickles.

They're softer than I imagined.

I'm glad he didn't get squashed.

Or eaten.

Oh, look at that.

Stars.

I didn't notice them before.

It's funny how people always strive for the most hyperbolic, poetical and grandiose terms when trying to describe stars and how far away they are. It's all vast empty reaches of space and aeons of light-years when all anyone really needs to say is they're a long way away.

A long way away is a long way.

But they're not really a long way away either.

They're a long time ago. They don't exist any more. Some of them went boom before Adam was a boy. What we're looking at are the memories of stars.

But they're beautiful just the same.

www.vintage-books.co.uk